This Book Belongs To

by L. Frank Baum
Illustrated by John R. Neill

Adventures Under the Sea!

L. Frank Baum is best known as the author of **The Wonderful Wizard of Oz** (1900) and its thirteen sequels. Baum's other fantasies, though less well known, are equally marvelous. **The Sea Fairies**, first published in 1911, has all the magic, excitement and fun for which Baum is so famous.

The Sea Fairies introduces us to Trot and Cap'n Bill, who appear in later Oz books. Their high-spirited adventures in the underwater kingdom of the Mermaids are captured in the numerous illustrations of Oz artist, John R. Neill.

Filled with fanciful characters and a touch of high adventure, **The Sea Fairies** is sure to delight the legion of fans who already love **The Wizard of Oz**!

An Underwater Classic!

SKY
ISLAND

SKY ISLAND

*Being the Further Exciting Adventures
of Trot and Cap'n Bill after Their
Visit to the Sea Fairies*

By

L. FRANK BAUM

AUTHOR OF THE SEA FAIRIES, THE EMERALD CITY OF OZ,
DOROTHY AND THE WIZARD IN OZ, OZMA OF OZ,
THE ROAD TO OZ, THE LAND OF OZ, ETC.

ILLUSTRATED BY
JOHN R. NEILL

———

BOOKS OF WONDER

COPYRIGHT 1912 BY L. FRANK BAUM

Books of Wonder
16 West 18th Street
New York, NY 10011

ISBN 0-929605-01-2 (pb)

ISBN 0-929605-02-0 (hc)

4 5 6 7 8 9 10

Books of Wonder is a registered trademark of Ozma, Inc.

TO
MY SISTER
MARY LOUISE BREWSTER

A LITTLE TALK TO MY READERS

WITH "The Sea Fairies," my book for 1911, I ventured into a new field of fairy literature and to my delight the book was received with much approval by my former readers, many of whom have written me that they like Trot "almost as well as Dorothy." As Dorothy was an old, old friend and Trot a new one, I think this is very high praise for Cap'n Bill's little companion. Cap'n Bill is also a new character who seems to have won approval, and so both Trot and the old sailor are again introduced in the present story, which may be called the second of the series of adventures of Trot and Cap'n Bill.

But you will recognize some other acquaintances in "Sky Island." Here, for instance, is Button-Bright, who once had an adventure with Dorothy in Oz, and without Button-Bright and his Magic Umbrella you will see that the story of " Sky Island" could never have been written. As Polychrome, the Rainbow's Daughter, lives in the sky, it is natural that Trot and Button-Bright meet her during their adventures there.

This story of Sky Island has astonished me considerably, and I think it will also astonish you. The sky country is certainly a remarkable fairyland, but after reading about it I am sure you will agree with me that our old Mother Earth is a very good place to live upon and that Trot and Button-Bright and Cap'n Bill were fortunate to get back to it again.

By the way, one of my little correspondents has suggested that I print my address in this book, so that the children may know where letters will reach me. I am doing this, as you see, and hope that many will write to me and tell me how they like "Sky Island." My greatest treasures are these letters from my readers and I am always delighted to receive them.

L. FRANK BAUM.

"OZCOT"
at HOLLYWOOD
in CALIFORNIA

LIST OF CHAPTERS

A MYSTERIOUS ARRIVAL

CHAPTER I.

"HELLO," said the boy.

"Hello," answered Trot, looking up surprised. "Where did you come from?"

"Philadelphia," said he.

"Dear me," said Trot; "you're a long way from home, then."

"'Bout as far as I can get, in this country," the boy replied, gazing out over the water. "Isn't this the Pacific Ocean?"

"Of course."

"Why of course?" he asked.

"Because it's the biggest lot of water in all the world."

"How do you know?"

"Cap'n Bill told me," she said.

"Who's Cap'n Bill?"

"An old sailorman who's a friend of mine. He lives at my house, too—the white house you see over there on the bluff."

"Oh; is that your home?"

"Yes," said Trot, proudly. "Isn't it pretty?"

"It's pretty small, seems to me," answered the boy.

"But it's big enough for mother and me, an' for Cap'n Bill," said Trot.

"Haven't you any father?"

"Yes, 'ndeed; Cap'n Griffith is my father; but he's gone, most of the time, sailin' on his ship. You mus' be a stranger in these parts, little boy, not to know 'bout Cap'n Griffith," she added, looking at her new acquaintance intently.

Trot wasn't very big herself, but the boy was not quite as big as Trot. He was thin, with a rather pale complexion and his blue eyes were round and earnest. He wore a blouse waist, a short jacket and knickerbockers. Under his arm he held an old umbrella that was as tall as he was. Its covering had once been of thick brown cloth, but the color had faded to a dull drab, except in the creases, and Trot thought it looked very old-fashioned and common. The handle, though, was really curious. It,was of wood and carved to resemble an elephant's head. The long trunk of the elephant was curved to make a crook for the handle. The eyes of the beast were small red stones, and it had two tiny tusks of ivory.

The boy's dress was rich and expensive, even to his fine silk stockings and tan shoes; but the umbrella looked old and disreputable.

"It isn't the rainy season now," remarked Trot, with a smile.

The boy glanced at his umbrella and hugged it tighter.

"No," he said; "but umbrellas are good for other things 'sides rain."

"'Fraid of gett'n' sun-struck?" asked Trot.

He shook his head, still gazing far out over the water.

"I don't b'lieve this is bigger than any other ocean," said he. "I can't see any more of it than I can of the Atlantic."

"You'd find out, if you had to sail across it," she declared.

"When I was in Chicago I saw Lake Michigan," he went on dreamily, "and it looked just as big as this water does."

"Looks don't count, with oceans," she asserted. "Your eyes can only see jus' so far, whether you're lookin' at a pond or a great sea."

"Then it doesn't make any difference how big an ocean is," he replied. "What are those buildings over there?" pointing to the right, along the shore of the bay.

"That's the town," said Trot. "Most of the people earn their living by fishing. The town is half a mile from here an' my house is almost a half mile the other way; so it's 'bout a mile from my house to the town."

The boy sat down beside her on the flat rock.

"Do you like girls?" asked Trot, making room for him.

"Not very well," the boy replied. "Some of 'em are pretty good fellows, but not many. The girls with brothers are bossy, an' the girls without brothers haven't any 'go' to 'em. But the world's full o' both kinds, and so I try to take 'em as they come. They can't help being girls, of course. Do you like boys?"

"When they don't put on airs, or get rough-house," replied Trot. "My 'sperience with boys is that they don't know much, but think they do."

"That's true," he answered. "I don't like boys much better than I do girls; but some are all right, and — you seem to be one of 'em."

"Much obliged," laughed Trot. "You aren't so bad, either, an' if we don't both turn out worse than we seem we ought to be friends."

He nodded, rather absently, and tossed a pebble into the water.

"Been to town?" he asked.

"Yes. Mother wanted some yarn from the store. She's knittin' Cap'n Bill a stocking."

"Doesn't he wear but one?"

"That's all. Cap'n Bill has one wooden leg," she explained. "That's why he don't sailor any more. I'm glad of it, 'cause Cap'n Bill knows ev'rything. I s'pose he knows more than anyone else in all the world."

16

"Whew!" said the boy; "that's taking a good deal for granted A one-legged sailor can't know much."

"Why not?" asked Trot, a little indignantly. "Folks don't learn things with their legs, do they?"

"No; but they can't get around, without legs, to find out things."

"Cap'n Bill got 'round lively 'nough once, when he had two meat legs," she said. "He's sailed to 'most ev'ry country on the earth, an' found out all that the people in 'em knew, and a lot besides. He was shipwrecked on a desert island, once, and another time a cannibal king tried to boil him for dinner, an' one day a shark chased him seven leagues through the water, an'—"

"What's a league?" asked the boy.

"It's a — a distance, like a mile is; but a league isn't a mile, you know."

"What is it, then?"

"You'll have to ask Cap'n Bill; he knows ever'thing."

"Not ever'thing," objected the boy. "I know some things Cap'n Bill don't know."

"If you do you're pretty smart," said Trot.

"No; I'm not smart. Some folks think I'm stupid. I guess I am. But I know a few things that are wonderful. Cap'n Bill may know more'n I do — a good deal more — but I'm sure he can't know the same things. Say, what's your name?"

"I'm Mayre Griffith; but ever'body calls me 'Trot.' It's a nickname I got when I was a baby, 'cause I trotted so fast when I walked, an' it seems to stick. What's *your* name?"

"Button-Bright."

"How did it happen?"

"How did what happen?"

"Such a funny name."

The boy scowled a little.

"Just like your own nickname happened," he answered gloomily. "My father once said I was bright as a button, an' it made ever'body laugh. So they always call me Button-Bright."

"What's your real name?" she inquired.

"Saladin Paracelsus de Lambertine Evagne von Smith."

"Guess I'll call you Button-Bright," said Trot, sighing. "The only other thing would be 'Salad,' an' I don't like salads. Don't you find it hard work to 'member all of your name?"

"I don't try to," he said. "There's a lot more of it, but I've forgotten the rest."

"Thank you," said Trot. "Oh, here comes Cap'n Bill!" as she glanced over her shoulder.

Button-Bright turned also and looked solemnly at the old sailor who came stumping along the path toward them. Cap'n Bill wasn't a very handsome man. He was old, not very tall, somewhat stout and chubby, with a round face, a bald head and a scraggly fringe of reddish whisker underneath his chin. But his blue eyes were frank and merry and his smile like a ray of sunshine. He wore a sailor shirt with a broad collar, a short peajacket and wide-bottomed sailor trousers, one leg of which covered his wooden limb but did not hide it. As he came "pegging" along the path, as he himself described his hobbling walk, his hands were pushed into his coat pockets, a pipe was in his mouth and his black neckscarf was fluttering behind him in the breeze like a sable banner.

Button-Bright liked the sailor's looks. There was something very winning — something jolly and care-free and honest and sociable — about the ancient seaman that made him everybody's friend; so the strange boy was glad to meet him.

"Well, well, Trot," he said, coming up, "is this the way you hurry to town?"

"No, for I'm on my way back," said she. "I did hurry when I was going, Cap'n Bill, but on my way home I sat down here to rest an' watch the gulls — the gulls seem awful busy to-day, Cap'n Bill — an' then I found this boy."

Cap'n Bill looked at the boy curiously.

"Don't think as ever I sawr him at the village," he remarked. "Guess as you're a stranger, my lad."

Button-Bright nodded.

"Hain't walked the nine mile from the railroad station, hev ye?" asked Cap'n Bill.

"No," said Button-Bright.

The sailor glanced around him.

"Don't see no waggin, er no autymob'l'," he added.

"No," said Button-Bright.

"Catch a ride wi' some one?"

Button-Bright shook his head.

"A boat can't land here; the rocks is too thick an' too sharp," continued Cap'n Bill, peering down toward the foot of the bluff on which they sat and against which the waves broke in foam.

"No," said Button-Bright; "I didn't come by water."

Trot laughed.

"He must 'a' dropped from the sky, Cap'n Bill!" she exclaimed.

Button-Bright nodded, very seriously.

"That's it," he said.

"Oh; a airship, eh?" cried Cap'n Bill, in surprise. "I've hearn tell o' them sky keeridges; someth'n' like flyin' autymob'l's, ain't they?"

"I don't know," said Button-Bright; "I've never seen one."

Both Trot and Cap'n Bill now looked at the boy in astonishment.

"Now, then, lemme think a minute," said the sailor, reflectively. "Here's a riddle for us to guess, Trot. He dropped from the sky, he says, an' yet he did'nt come in a airship!

"'Riddlecum, riddlecum ree;
What can the answer be?'"

Trot looked the boy over carefully. She didn't see any wings on him. The only queer thing about him was his big umbrella.

"Oh!" she said suddenly, clapping her hands together; "I know now."

"Do you?" asked Cap'n Bill, doubtfully. "Then you're some smarter ner I am, mate."

"He sailed down with the umbrel!" she cried. "He used his umbrel as a para—para—"

"Shoot," said Cap'n Bill. "They're called parashoots, mate; but why, I can't say. Did you drop down in that way, my lad?" he asked the boy.

"Yes," said Button-Bright; "that was the way."

"But how did you get up there?" asked Trot. "You had to get up in the air before you could drop down, an'—oh, Cap'n Bill! he says he's from Phillydelfy, which is a big city way at the other end of America."

"Are you?" asked the sailor, surprised.

Button-Bright nodded again.

"I ought to tell you my story," he said, "and then you'd understand. But I'm afraid you won't believe me, and—" he suddenly broke off and looked toward the white house in the distance—"Didn't you say you lived over there?" he inquired.

Sky Island

"Yes," said Trot. "Won't you come home with us?"

"I'd like to," replied Button-Bright.

"All right; let's go, then," said the girl, jumping up.

The three walked silently along the path. The old sailorman had refilled his pipe and lighted it again, and he smoked thoughtfully as he pegged along beside the children.

"Know anyone around here?" he asked Button-Bright.

"No one but you two," said the boy, following after Trot, with his umbrella tucked carefully underneath his arm.

"And you don't know us very well," remarked Cap'n Bill. "Seems to me you're pretty young to be travelin' so far from home, an' among strangers; but I won't say anything more till we've heard your story. Then, if you need my advice, or Trot's advice—she's a wise little girl, fer her size, Trot is—we'll freely give it an' be glad to help you."

"Thank you," replied Button-Bright; "I need a lot of things, I'm sure, and p'raps advice is one of 'em."

THE MAGIC UMBRELLA

CHAPTER 2.

WHEN they reached the neat frame cottage which stood on a high bluff a little back from the sea and was covered with pretty green vines, a woman came to the door to meet them. She seemed motherly and good and when she saw Button-Bright she exclaimed:

"Goodness me! who's this you've got, Trot?"

"It's a boy I've just found," explained the girl. "He lives way off in Phillydelphy."

"Mercy sakes alive!" cried Mrs. Griffith, looking into his upturned face; "I don't believe he's had a bite to eat since he started. Ain't you hungry, child?"

"Yes," said Button-Bright.

"Run, Trot, an' get two slices o' bread-an'-butter," commanded Mrs. Griffith. "Cut 'em thick, dear, an' use plenty of butter."

"Sugar on 'em?" asked Trot, turning to obey.

"No," said Button-Bright, "just bread-an'-butter's good enough when you're hungry, and it takes time to spread sugar on."

"We'll have supper in an hour," observed Trot's mother, briskly; "but a hungry child can't wait a whole hour, I'm sure. What are you grinning at, Cap'n Bill? How dare you laugh when I'm talking? Stop it this minute, you old pirate, or I'll know the reason why!"

"I didn't, mum," said Cap'n Bill, meekly, "I on'y—"

"Stop right there, sir! How dare you speak when I'm talking?" She turned to Button-Bright and her tone changed to one of much gentleness as she said: "Come in the house, my poor boy, an' rest yourself. You seem tired out. Here, give me that clumsy umbrella."

"No, please," said Button-Bright, holding the umbrella tighter.

"Then put it in the rack behind the door," she urged.

The boy seemed a little frightened.

"I—I'd rather keep it with me, if you please," he pleaded.

"Never mind," Cap'n Bill ventured to say, "it won't worry him so much to hold the umbrella, mum, as to let it go. Guess he's afraid he'll lose it, but it ain't any great shakes, to my notion. Why, see here, Butt'n-Bright, we've got half-a-dozen umbrels in the closet that's better ner yours."

"Perhaps," said the boy. "Yours may look a heap better, sir, but — I'll keep this one, if you please."

"Where did you get it?" asked Trot, appearing just then with a plate of bread-and-butter.

"It — it belongs in our family," said Button-Bright, beginning to eat and speaking between bites. "This umbrella has been in our family years, an' years, an' years. But it was

tucked away up in our attic an' no one ever used it 'cause it wasn't pretty."

"Don't blame 'em much," remarked Cap'n Bill, gazing at it curiously; "it's a pretty old-lookin' bumbershoot." They were all seated in the vine-shaded porch of the cottage — all but Mrs. Griffith, who had gone into the kitchen to look after the supper — and Trot was on one side of the boy, holding the plate for him, while Cap'n Bill sat on the other side.

"It *is* old," said Button-Bright. "One of my great-great-grandfathers was a Knight — an Arabian Knight — and it was he who first found this umbrella."

"An Arabian Night!" exclaimed Trot; "why, that was a magic night, wasn't it?"

"There's diff'rent sorts o' nights, mate," said the sailor, "an' the knight Button-Bright means ain't the same night you mean. Soldiers used to be called knights, but that were in the dark ages, I guess, an' likely 'nough Butt'n-Bright's great-gran'ther were that sort of a knight."

"But he said an Arabian Knight," persisted Trot.

"Well, if he went to Araby, or was born there, he'd be an Arabian Knight, wouldn't he? The lad's gran'ther were prob'ly a furriner, an' yours an' mine were, too, Trot, if you go back far enough; for Ameriky wasn't diskivered in them days."

"There!" said Trot, triumphantly, "didn't I tell you, Button-Bright, that Cap'n Bill knows ever'thing?"

"He knows a lot, I expect," soberly answered the boy, finishing the last slice of bread-and-butter and then looking at the empty plate with a sigh; "but if he really knows everthing he knows about the Magic Umbrella, so I won't have to tell you anything about it."

Chapter Two

"Magic!" cried Trot, with big, eager eyes; "did you say *Magic* Umbrel, Button-Bright?"

"I said 'Magic.' But none of our family knew it was a Magic Umbrella till I found it out for myself. You 're the first people I 've told the secret to," he added, glancing into their faces rather uneasily.

"Glory me!" exclaimed the girl, clapping her hands in ecstacy; " it must be jus' *elegant* to have a Magic Umbrel! "

Cap'n Bill coughed. He had a way of coughing when he was suspicious.

"Magic," he observed gravely, "was once lyin' 'round loose in the world. That was in the Dark Ages, I guess, when the magic Arabian Nights was. But the light o' Civilization has skeered it away long ago, an' magic's been a lost art since long afore you an' I was born, Trot."

"I know that fairies still live," said Trot, reflectively. She did n't like to contradict Cap'n Bill, who knew "ever'-thing."

"So do I," added Button-Bright. "And I know there 's magic still in the world—or in my umbrella, anyhow."

" Tell us about it! " begged the girl, excitedly.

"Well," said the boy, "I found it all out by accident. It rained in Philadelphia for three whole days, and all the umbrellas in our house were carried out by the family, and lost or mislaid, or something, so that when I wanted to go to Uncle Bob's house, which is at Germantown, there was n't

27

an umbrella to be found. My governess wouldn't let me go without one, and —"

"Oh," said Trot; "do you have a governess?"

"Yes; but I don't like her; she's cross. She said I couldn't go to Uncle Bob's because I had no umbrella. Instead she told me to go up in the attic and play. I was sorry 'bout that, but I went up in the attic and pretty soon I found in a corner this old umbrella. I didn't care how it looked. It was whole and strong and big, and would keep me from getting wet on the way to Uncle Bob's. So off I started for the car, but I found the streets awful muddy, and once I stepped in a mud-hole way up to my ankle.

" ' Gee! ' I said, ' I wish I could fly through the air to Uncle Bob's.'

"I was holding up the open umbrella when I said that, and as soon as I spoke, the umbrella began lifting me up into the air. I was awful scared, at first, but I held on tight to the handle and it didn't pull very much, either. I was going pretty fast, for when I looked down, all the big buildings were sliding past me so swift that it made me dizzy, and before I really knew what had happened the umbrella settled down and stood me on my feet at Uncle Bob's front gate.

"I didn't tell anybody about the wonderful thing that had happened, 'cause I thought no one would believe me. Uncle Bob looked sharp at the thing an' said: ' Button-Bright, how did your father happen to let you take that umbrella?'

Chapter Two

' He did n't,' I said. ' Father was away at the office, so I found it in the attic an' I jus' took it.' Then Uncle Bob shook his head an' said I ought to leave it alone. He said it was a fam'ly relic that had been handed down from father to son for many generations. But I told him my father had never handed it to me, though I 'm his son. Uncle Bob said our fam'ly always believed that it brought 'em good luck to own this umbrella. He could n't say why, not knowing its early history, but he was afraid that if I lost the umbrella bad luck would happen to us. So he made me go right home to put the umbrella back where I got it. I was sorry Uncle Bob was so cross, and I did n't want to go home yet, where the governess was crosser 'n he was. I wonder why folks get cross when it rains? But by that time it had stopped raining, for awhile, anyhow, and Uncle Bob told me to go straight home and put the umbrella in the attic an' never touch it again.

"When I was around the corner I thought I'd see if I could fly as I had before. I 'd heard of Buffalo, but I did n't know just where it was; so I said to the umbrella: ' Take me to Buffalo.'

"Up in the air I went, just as soon as I said it, and the umbrella sailed so fast that I felt as if I was in a gale of wind. It was a long, long trip, and I got awful tired holding onto the handle, but just as I thought I 'd have to let go I began to drop down slowly, and then I found myself in the streets of

31

a big city. I put down the umbrella and asked a man what the name of the city was, and he said 'Buffalo.'"

"How wonderful!" gasped Trot. Cap'n Bill kept on smoking and said nothing.

"It was magic, I'm sure," said Button-Bright. "It surely could n't have been anything else."

"P'raps," suggested Trot, "the umbrella can do other magic things."

"No," said the boy; "I've tried it. When I landed in Buffalo I was hot and thirsty. I had ten cents, car fare, but I was afraid to spend it. So I held up the umbrella and wished I had an ice-cream soda; but I did n't get it. Then I wished for a nickel to buy an ice-cream soda with; but I did n't get that, either. I got frightened and was afraid the umbrella did n't have any magic left, so to try it I said: 'Take me to Chicago.' I did n't want to go to Chicago, but that was the first place I thought of, and so I said it. Up again I flew, swifter than a bird, and I soon saw this was going to be another long journey; so I called out to the umbrella: 'Never mind; stop! I guess I won't go to Chicago. I've changed my mind, so take me home again.' But the umbrella would n't. It kept right on flying and I shut my eyes and held on. At last I landed in Chicago, and then I was in a pretty fix. It was nearly dark and I was too tired and hungry to make the trip home again. I knew I'd get an awful scolding, too, for running away and taking the family luck with me, so I thought that as long as I was in for it I'd better see a good deal of the country while I had the chance. I would n't be allowed to come away again, you know."

"No, of course not," said Trot.

"I bought some buns and milk with my ten cents and then I walked around the streets of Chicago for a time and afterward slept on a bench in one of the parks. In the morning I tried to get the umbrella to give me a magic breakfast, but it won't do anything but fly. I went to a house and asked a woman for something to eat and she gave me all I wanted and advised me to go straight home before my mother worried about me. She did n't know I lived in Philadelphia. That was this morning."

"This mornin'!" exclaimed Cap'n Bill. "Why, lad, it takes three or four days for the railroad trains to get to this coast from Chicago."

"I know," replied Button-Bright, "but I did n't come on a railroad train. This umbrella goes faster than any train ever did. This morning I flew from Chicago to Denver, but no one there would give me any lunch. A policeman said he'd put me in jail if he caught me begging, so I got away and told the umbrella to take me to the Pacific Ocean. When I stopped I landed over there by the big rock. I shut up the umbrella and saw a girl sitting on the rock, so I went up and spoke to her. That's all."

"Goodness me!" said Trot; "if that isn't a fairy story I never heard one."

"It *is* a fairy story," agreed Button-Bright. "Anyhow, it's a magic story, and the funny part of it is, it's true. I hope you believe me; but I don't know as I'd believe it myself, if it hadn't been me that it happened to."

"I believe ev'ry word of it!" declared Trot, earnestly.

"As fer me," said Cap'n Bill slowly, "I'm goin' to believe it, too, by'm'by, when I've seen the umbrel fly once."

"You'll see me fly away with it," asserted the boy. "But at present it's pretty late in the day, and Philadelphia is a good way off. Do you s'pose, Trot, your mother would let me stay here all night?"

"Course she would!" answered Trot. "We've got an extra room with a nice bed in it, and we'd love to have you stay—just as long as you want to—wouldn't we, Cap'n Bill?"

"Right you are, mate," replied the old man, nodding his bald head. "Whether the umbrel is magic or not, Butt'n-Bright is welcome."

Mrs. Griffith came out soon after, and seconded the invitation, so the boy felt quite at home in the little cottage. It was not long before supper was on the table and in spite of all the bread-and-butter he had eaten Button-Bright had a fine appetite for the good things Trot's mother had cooked. Mrs. Griffith was very kind to the children, but not quite so agreeable toward poor Cap'n Bill. When the old sailorman at one time spilled some tea on the tablecloth Trot's mother flew angry and gave the culprit such a tongue-lashing that Button-Bright was sorry for him. But Cap'n Bill was meek and made no reply. "He's used to it, you know," whispered Trot to her new friend; and, indeed, Cap'n Bill took it all cheerfully and never minded a bit.

Then it came Trot's turn to get a scolding. When she opened the parcel she had bought at the village it was found she had selected the wrong color of yarn, and Mrs. Griffith was so provoked that Trot's scolding was almost as severe as that of Cap'n Bill. Tears came to the little girl's eyes, and to comfort her the boy promised to take her to the village next morning with his magic umbrella, so she could exchange the yarn for the right color.

Trot quickly brightened at this promise, although Cap'n Bill looked grave and shook his head solemnly. When supper was over and Trot had helped with the dishes she joined Button-Bright and the sailorman on the little porch again. Dusk had fallen and the moon was just rising. They all sat in silence for a time and watched the silver trail that topped the crests of the waves far out to sea.

"Oh, Button-Bright!" cried the little girl, presently; "I'm so glad you're going to let me fly with you—way to town and back—to-morrow. Won't it be fine, Cap'n Bill?"

"Dunno, Trot," said he. "I can't figger how both o' you can hold on to the handle o' that umbrel."

Trot's face fell.

"I'll hold on to the handle," said Button-Bright, "and she can hold on to me. It doesn't pull hard at all. You've no idea how easy it is to fly that way—after you get used to it."

"But Trot ain't used to it," objected the sailor. "If she happened to lose her hold and let go, it's good-bye Trot. I don't like to risk it, for Trot's my chum, an' I can't afford to lose her."

"Can't you tie us together, then?" asked the boy.

"We'll see; we'll see," replied Cap'n Bill, and began to think very deeply. He forgot that he didn't believe the umbrella could fly, and after Button-Bright and Trot had both gone to bed the old sailor went out into the shed and worked awhile before he, too, turned into his "bunk." The sandman wasn't around and Cap'n Bill lay awake for hours thinking of the strange tale of the Magic Umbrella before he finally sank into slumber. Then he dreamed about it, and waking or dreaming he found the tale hard to believe.

A WONDERFUL EXPERIENCE

CHAPTER 3.

THEY had early breakfasts at Trot's house, because they all went to bed early and it is possible to sleep only a certain number of hours if one is healthy in body and mind. And right after breakfast Trot claimed Button-Bright's promise to take her to town with the Magic Umbrella.

"Any time suits me," said the boy. He had taken his precious umbrella to bed with him and even carried it to the breakfast table, where he stood it between his knees as he ate; so now he held it close to him and said he was ready to fly at a moment's notice. This confidence impressed Cap'n Bill, who said with a sigh:

"Well, if you *must* go, Trot, I've pervided a machine that'll carry you both comf'table. I'm summat of an inventor myself, though there ain't any magic about me."

Then he brought from the shed the contrivance he had made the night before. It was merely a swing seat. He had

37

taken a wide board that was just long enough for both the boy and girl to sit upon, and had bored six holes in it — two holes at each end ánd two in the middle. Through these holes he had run stout ropes in such a way that the seat could not turn and the occupants could hold on to the ropes on either side of them. The ropes were all knotted together at

the top, where there was a loop that could be hooked upon the crooked handle of the umbrella.

Button-Bright and Trot both thought Cap'n Bill's invention very clever. The sailor placed the board upon the ground while they sat in their places, Button-Bright at the right of Trot, and then the boy hooked the rope loop to the handle of the umbrella, which he spread wide open.

Chapter Three

"I want to go to the town over yonder," he said, pointing with his finger to the roofs of the houses that showed around the bend in the cliff.

At once the umbrella rose into the air; slowly, at first, but quickly gathering speed. Trot and Button-Bright held fast to the ropes and were carried along very easily and comfortably. It seemed scarcely a minute before they were in the town, and when the umbrella set them down just in front of the store — for it seemed to know just where they wanted to go — a wondering crowd gathered around them. Trot ran in and changed the yarn, while Button-Bright stayed outside and stared at the people who stared at him. They asked questions, too, wanting to know what sort of an aëroplane this was, and where his power was stored, and lots of other things; but the boy answered not a word. When the little girl came back and took her seat Button-Bright said:

"I want to go to Trot's house."

The simple villagers could not understand how the umbrella suddenly lifted the two children into the air and carried them away. They had read of airships, but here was something wholly beyond their comprehension.

Cap'n Bill had stood in front of the house, watching with a feeling akin to bewilderment the flight of the Magic Umbrella. He could follow its course until it descended in the village and he was so amazed and absorbed that his pipe went out. He had not moved from his position when the um-

39

brella started back. The sailor's big blue eyes watched it draw near and settle down with its passengers upon just the spot it had started from.

Trot was joyous and greatly excited.

"Oh, Cap'n, it's gal-lor-ious!" she cried in ecstasy. "It beats ridin' in a boat or — or — in anything else. You feel so light an' free an' — an' — glad! I'm sorry the trip didn't last longer, though. Only trouble is, you go too fast."

Button-Bright was smiling contentedly. He had proved to both Trot and Cap'n Bill that he had told the truth about the Magic Umbrella, however marvelous his tale had seemed to them.

"I'll take you on another trip, if you like," said he, "I'm in no hurry to go home and if you will let me stay with you another day we can make two or three little trips with the family luck."

"You mus' stay a whole week," said Trot, decidedly. "An' you mus' take Cap'n Bill for an air-ride, too."

"Oh, Trot! I dunno as I'd like it," protested Cap'n Bill, nervously.

"Yes, you would. You're sure to like it."

"I guess I'm too heavy," he said.

"I'm sure the umbrella could carry twenty people, if they could be fastened to the handle," said Button-Bright.

"Solid land's pretty good to hold on to," decided Cap'n Bill. "A rope might break, you know."

Chapter Three

"Oh, Cap'n Bill! You're scared stiff," said Trot.

"I ain't, mate; it ain't that at all. But I don't see that human critters has any call to fly in the air, anyhow. The air were made for the birds, an'—an' muskeeters, an'—"

"An' flyin'-fishes," added Trot. "I know all that, Cap'n; but why wasn't it made for humans, too, if they can manage to fly in it? We breathe the air, an' we can breathe it high up, just as well as down on the earth."

"Seein' as you like it so much, Trot, it would be cruel for me to go with Butt'n-Bright an' leave you at home," said the sailor. "When I were younger—which is ancient history— an' afore I had a wooden leg, I could climb a ship's ropes with the best of 'em, an' walk out on a boom, or stand atop a mast. So you know very well I ain't skeert about the high-upness."

"Why can't we all go together?" asked the boy. "Make another seat, Cap'n, and swing it right under ours; then we can all three ride anywhere we want to go."

"Yes, do!" exclaimed Trot. "And, see here, Cap'n; let's take a day off and have a picnic. Mother is a little cross, to-day, and she wants to finish knitting your new stockin'; so I guess she'll be glad to get rid of us."

"Where'll we go?" he asked, shifting on his wooden leg uneasily.

"Anywhere; I don't care. There'll be the air-ride there, an' the air-ride back, an' that's the main thing with *me*. If

41

you say you'll go, Cap'n, I'll run in an' pack a basket of lunch."

"How'll we carry it?"

"Swing it to the bottom of your seat."

The old sailor stood silent a moment. He really longed to take the air-ride but was fearful of danger. However, Trot had gone safely to town and back and had greatly enjoyed the experience.

"All right," he said; "I'll risk it, mate, although I guess I'm an old fool for temptin' fate by tryin' to make a bird o' myself. Get the lunch, Trot, if your mother 'll let you have it, and I'll rig up the seat."

He went into the shed and Trot went to her mother. Mrs. Griffith, busy with her work, knew nothing of what was going on in regard to the flight of the Magic Umbrella. She never objected when Trot wanted to go away with Cap'n Bill for a day's picnicking. She knew the child was perfectly safe with the old sailor, who cared for Trot even better than her mother would have done. If she had asked any questions to-day, and had found out they intended to fly in the air, she might have seriously objected; but Mrs. Griffith had her mind on other things and merely told the girl to take what she wanted from the cupboard and not bother her. So Trot, remembering that Button-Bright would be with them and had proved himself to be a hearty eater, loaded the basket with all the good things she could find.

Chapter Three

By the time she came out, lugging the basket with both hands, Cap'n Bill appeared with the new seat he had made for his own use, which he attached by means of ropes to the double seat of the boy and girl.

"Now, then, where'll we go?" asked Trot.

"Anywhere suits me," replied Cap'n Bill.

They had walked to the high bluff overlooking the sea, where a gigantic acacia tree stood on the very edge. A seat had been built around the trunk of the tree, for this was a favorite spot for Trot and Cap'n Bill to sit and talk and watch the fleet of fishing boats sail to and from the village.

When they came to this tree Trot was still trying to think of the most pleasant place to picnic. She and Cap'n Bill had been every place that was desirable and near by, but to-day they didn't want a near-by spot. They must decide upon one far enough away to afford them a fine trip through the air. Looking far out over the Pacific, the girl's eyes fell upon a dim island lying on the horizon line — just where the sky and water seemed to meet — and the sight gave her an idea.

"Oh, Cap'n Bill!" she exclaimed, "let's go to that island for our picnic. We've never been there yet, you know."

The sailor shook his head.

"It's a good many miles away, Trot," he said; "further than it looks to be, from here."

"That won't matter," remarked Button-Bright; "the umbrella will carry us there in no time."

43

Sky Island

"Let's go!" repeated Trot. "We'll never have another such chance, Cap'n. It's too far to sail or row, and I've always wanted to visit th.it island."

"What's the name of it?" inquired Button-Bright, while the sailor hesitated how to decide.

"Oh, it's got an awful hard name to pernounce," replied the girl, "so Cap'n Bill and I jus' call it 'Sky Island,' 'cause it looks as if it was half in the sky. We've been told it's a very pretty island, and a few people live there and keep cows and goats, and fish for a living. There are woods and pastures and springs of clear water, and I'm sure we would find it a fine place for a picnic."

"If anything happened on the way," observed Cap'n Bill, "we'd drop in the water."

"Of course," said Trot; "and if anything happened while we were flyin' over the land we'd drop there. But nothing's goin' to happen, Cap'n. Did n't Button-Bright come safe all the way from Philydelfy?"

"I think I'd like to go to Sky Island," said the boy. "I've always flown above the land, so far, and it will be something new to fly over the ocean."

"All right; I'm agree'ble," decided Cap'n Bill. "But afore we starts on such a long journey, s'pose we make a little trial trip along the coast. I want to see if the new seat fits me, an' make certain the umbrel will carry all three of us."

"Very well," said Button-Bright. "Where shall we go?"

Chapter Three

"Let's go as far as Smuggler's Cove, an' then turn 'round an' come back. If all's right an' shipshape, then we can start for the island."

They put the broad double seat on the ground and then the boy and girl sat in their places and Button-Bright spread open the Magic Umbrella. Cap'n Bill sat in his seat just in front of them, all being upon the ground.

"Don't we look funny?" said Trot, with a chuckle of glee. "But hold fast the ropes, Cap'n, an' take care of your wooden leg."

Button-Bright addressed the umbrella, speaking to it very respectfully, for it was a thing to inspire awe.

"I want to go as far as Smuggler's Cove, and then turn around in the air and come back here," he said.

At once the umbrella rose into the air, lifting after it, first the seat in which the children sat, and then Cap'n Bill's seat.

"Don't kick your heels, Trot!" creid the sailor in a voice that proved he was excited by his novel experience; "you might bump me in the nose."

"All right," she called back; "I'll be careful."

It was really a wonderful, exhilarating ride, and Cap'n Bill was n't long making up his mind he liked the sensation. When about fifty feet above the ground the umbrella began moving along the coast toward Smuggler's Cove, which it soon reached. Looking downward, Cap'n Bill suddenly exclaimed:

"Why, there's a boat cast loose, an' it's goin' to smash on the rocks. Hold on a minute, Butt'n-Bright, till we can land an' drag it ashore."

"Hold on a minute, Umbrella!" cried the boy.

But the Magic Umbrella kept steadily upon its way. It made a circle over the Cove and then started straight back the way it had come.

"It's no use, sir," said Button-Bright to the sailor. "If I once tell it to go to a certain place, the umbrella will go there, and nowhere else. I've found that out before this. You simply *can't* stop it."

"Won't let you change your mind, eh?" replied Cap'n Bill. "Well, that has its advantidges, an' its disadvantidges. If your ol' umbrel hadn't been so obstinate we could have saved that boat."

"Never mind," said Trot, briskly; "here we are safe back again. Wasn't it jus' the — the fascinatingest ride you ever took, Cap'n?"

"It's pretty good fun," admitted Cap'n Bill. "Beats them aëroplanes an' things all holler, 'cause it don't need any regulatin'."

"If we're going to that island we may as well start right away," said Button-Bright, when they had safely landed.

"All right; I'll tie on the lunch-basket," answered the sailor. He fastened it so it would swing underneath his own seat and then they all took their places again.

46

"Ready?" asked the boy.

"Let 'er go, my lad."

"I want to go to Sky Island," said Button-Bright to the umbrella, using the name Trot had given him.

The umbrella started promptly. It rose higher than before, carrying the three voyagers with it, and then started straight away over the ocean.

THE ISLAND IN THE SKY

CHAPTER 4.

THEY clung tightly to the ropes, but the breeze was with them, so after a few moments, when they became accustomed to the motion, they began to enjoy the ride immensely.

Larger and larger grew the island, and although they were headed directly toward it, the umbrella seemed to rise higher and higher into the air the farther it traveled. They had not journeyed ten minutes before they came directly over the island, and looking down they could see the forests and meadows far below them. But the umbrella kept up its rapid flight.

"Hold on, there!" cried Cap'n Bill. "If it ain't keerful the ol' thing will pass way by the island."

"I—I'm sure it has passed it already," exclaimed Trot. "What's wrong, Button-Bright? Why don't we stop?"

Button-Bright seemed astonished too.

"Perhaps I didn't say it right," he replied, after a

moment's thought. Then, looking up at the umbrella, he repeated, distinctly: "I said I wanted to go to Sky Island! Sky Island; don't you understand?"

The umbrella swept steadily along, getting farther and farther out to sea and rising higher and higher toward the clouds.

"Mack'rel an' herrings!" roared Cap'n Bill, now really frightened; "ain't there any blamed way at all to stop her?"

"None that I know of," said Button-Bright, anxiously.

"P'raps," said Trot, after a pause during which she tried hard to think, "p'raps 'Sky Island' isn't the name of that island, at all."

"Why, we know very well it ain't the name of it," yelled Cap'n Bill, from below. "We jus' called it that 'cause its right name is too hard to say."

"That's the whole trouble, then," returned Button-Bright. "Somewhere in the world there's a real Sky Island, and having told the Magic Umbrella to take us there, it's going to do so."

"Well, I declare!" gasped the sailorman; "can't we land anywhere else?"

"Not unless you care to tumble off," said the boy. "I've told the umbrella to take us to Sky Island, so that's the exact place we're bound for. I'm sorry. It was your fault for giving me the wrong name."

49

Sky Island

They glided along in silence for a while. The island was now far behind them, growing small in the distance.

"Where do you s'pose the real Sky Island can be?" asked Trot presently.

"We can't tell anything about it until we get there," Button-Bright answered. "Seems to me I've heard of the Isle of Skye, but that's over in Great Britain, somewhere the other side of the world; and it is n't Sky Island, anyhow."

"This miser'ble ol' umbrel is too pertic'ler," growled Cap'n Bill. "It won't let you change your mind an' it goes ezzac'ly where you say."

"If it did n't," said Trot, "we'd never know where we were going."

"We don't know now," said the sailor. "One thing's certain, folks: we're gett'n' a long way from home."

"And see how the clouds are rolling just above us," remarked the boy, who was almost as uneasy as Cap'n Bill.

"We're in the sky, all right," said the girl. "If there could be an island up here, among the clouds, I'd think it was there we're going."

"Could n't there be one?" asked Button-Bright. "Why could n't there be an island in the sky that would be named Sky Island?"

"Of course not!" declared Cap'n Bill. "There would n't be anything to hold it up, you know."

"What's holding *us* up?" asked Trot.

50

"Magic, I guess."

"Then magic might hold an island in the sky. . . . Whee-e-e-e! what a black cloud!"

It grew suddenly dark, for they were rushing through a thick cloud that rolled around them in billows. Trot felt little drops of moisture striking her face and knew her clothing was getting damp and soggy.

"It's a rain cloud," she said to Button-Bright, "and it seems like an awful big one, 'cause it takes so long for us to pass through it."

The umbrella never hesitated a moment. It made a path through the length of the heavy black cloud at last and carried its passengers into a misty, billowy bank of white, which seemed as soft and fleecy as a lady's veil. When this broke away they caught sight of a majestic rainbow spanning the heavens, its gorgeous colors glinting brightly in the sun, its arch perfect and unbroken from end to end. But it was only a glimpse they had, for quickly they dove into another bank of clouds and the rainbow disappeared.

Here the clouds were not black, nor heavy, but they assumed queer shapes. Some were like huge ships, some like forest trees, and others piled themselves into semblances of turreted castles and wonderful palaces. The shapes shifted here and there continually and the voyagers began to be bewildered by the phantoms.

"Seems to me we're goin' down," called Trot.

"Down where?" asked Cap'n Bill.

"Who knows?" said Button-Bright. "But we're dropping, all right."

It was a gradual descent. The Magic Umbrella maintained a uniform speed, swift and unfaltering, but its path through the heavens was now in the shape of an arch, as a flying arrow falls. The queer shapes of the clouds continued for some time, and once or twice Trot was a little frightened when a monstrous airy dragon passed beside them, or a huge giant stood upon a peak of cloud and stared savagely at the intruders into his domain. But none of these fanciful, vapory creatures seemed inclined to molest them or to interfere with their flight and after a while the umbrella dipped below this queer cloudland and entered a clear space where the sky was of an exquisite blue color.

"Oh, look!" called Cap'n Bill. "There's land below us."

The boy and girl leaned over and tried to see this land, but Cap'n Bill was also leaning over and his big body hid all that was just underneath them.

"Is it an island?" asked Trot, anxiously.

"Seems so," the old sailor replied. "The blue is around all one side of it an' a pink sunshine around the other side. There's a big cloud just over the middle; but I guess it's surely an island, Trot, an' bein' as it's in the sky, it's likely to be Sky Island."

"Then we shall land there," said the boy confidently. "I knew the umbrella couldn't make a mistake."

Presently Cap'n Bill spoke again.

"We're goin' down on the blue part o' the island," he said. "I can see trees, an' ponds, an' houses. Hold tight, Trot! Hold tight, Butt'n-Bright! I'm afeared we're a-goin' to bump somethin'!"

They were certainly dropping very quickly, now, and the rush of air made their eyes fill with water, so that they could not see much below them. Suddenly the basket that was dangling below Cap'n Bill's seat struck something with a loud thud and this was followed by a yell of anger. Cap'n Bill sat flat upon the ground, landing with a force that jarred the sailorman and made his teeth click together, while down

53

upon him came the seat that Trot and Button-Bright occupied, so that for a moment they were all tangled up.

"Get off from me! Get off from my feet, I say!" cried an excited voice. "What in the Sky do you mean by sitting on my feet? Get off! Get off at once!"

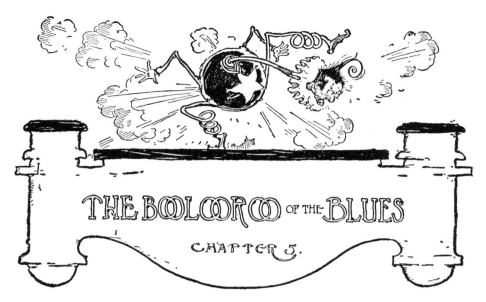

THE BOOLOOROO OF THE BLUES

CHAPTER 5.

CAP'N BILL suspected that these remarks were addressed to him, but he couldn't move just then because the seat was across him, and a boy and girl were sprawling on the seat. As the Magic Umbrella was now as motionless as any ordinary umbrella might be, Button-Bright first released the catch and closed it up, after which he unhooked the crooked handle from the rope and rose to his feet. Trot had managed by this time to stand up and she pulled the board off from Cap'n Bill. All this time the shrill, excited voice was loudly complaining because the sailor was on his feet, and Trot looked to see who was making the protest, while Cap'n Bill rolled over and got on his hands and knees so he could pull his meat leg and his wooden leg into an upright position, which wasn't a very easy thing to do.

Button-Bright and Trot were staring with all their might at the queerest person they had ever seen. They decided it must be a man, because he had two long legs, a body as round as a ball, a neck like an ostrich and a comical little head set on the top of it. But the most curious thing about him was his skin, which was of a lovely sky-blue tint. His eyes were also sky-blue, and his hair, which was trained straight up and ended in a curl at the top of his head, was likewise blue in color and matched his skin and his eyes. He wore tight-fitting clothes made of sky-blue silk, with a broad blue ruffle around his long neck, and on his breast glittered a magnificent jewel in the form of a star, set with splendid blue stones.

If the blue man astonished the travelers they were no less surprised by his surroundings, for look where they might, everything they beheld was of the same blue color as the sky above. They seemed to have landed in a large garden, surrounded by a high wall of blue stone. The trees were all blue, the grass was blue, the flowers were blue and even the pebbles in the paths were blue. There were many handsomely carved benches and seats of blue wood scattered about the garden, and near them stood a fountain, made of blue marble, which shot lovely sprays of blue water into the blue air.

But the angry inhabitant of this blue place would not permit them to look around them in peace, for as soon as Cap'n Bill rolled off his toes he began dancing around in an excited way and saying very disrespectful things of his visitors.

"You brutes! you apes! you miserable white-skinned creatures! How dare you come into my garden and knock me on the head with that awful basket and then fall on my toes and cause me pain and suffering? How dare you, I say? Don't you know you will be punished for your impudence? Don't you know the Boolooroo of the Blues will have revenge? I can have you patched for this insult, and I will —just as sure as I'm the Royal Boolooroo of Sky Island!"

"Oh, is this Sky Island, then?" asked Trot.

"Of course it's Sky Island. What else could it be? And I'm its Ruler—its King—its sole Royal Potentate and Dictator. Behold in the Personage you have injured the Mighty Quitey Righty Boolooroo of the Blues!" Here he strutted around in a very pompous manner and wagged his little head contemptuously at them.

"Glad to meet you, sir," said Cap'n Bill. "I allus had a likin' for kings, bein' as they're summat unusual. Please 'scuse me for a-sittin' on your royal toes, not knowin' as your toes were there."

"I won't excuse you!" roared the Boolooroo. "But I'll punish you. You may depend upon that."

"Seems to me," said Trot, "you're actin' rather imperlite to strangers. If anyone comes to our country to visit us, we always treat 'em decent."

"*Your* country!" exclaimed the Boolooroo, looking at them more carefully and seeming interested in their appearance. "Where in the Sky did you come from, then, and where is your country located?"

"We live on the Earth, when we're at home," replied the girl.

"The Earth? Nonsense! I've heard of the Earth, my child, but it isn't inhabited. No one can live there because it's just a round, cold, barren ball of mud and water," declared the Blueskin.

"Oh, you're wrong about that," said Button-Bright.

"You surely are," added Cap'n Bill.

"Why, we live there ourselves," cried Trot.

"I don't believe it. I believe you are living in Sky Island, where you have no right to be, with your horrid white skins. And you've intruded into the private garden of the palace of the Greatly Stately Irately Boolooroo, which is a criminal offense; and you've bumped my head with your basket and smashed my toes with your boards and bodies, which is a crime unparalleled in all the history of Sky Island! Aren't you sorry for yourselves?"

"I'm sorry for you," replied Trot, "'cause you don't seem to know the proper way to treat visitors. But we won't stay long. We'll go home, pretty soon."

"Not until you have been punished!" exclaimed the Boolooroo, sternly. "You are my prisoners."

"Beg parding, your Majesty," said Cap'n Bill, "but you're takin' a good deal for granted. We've tried to be friendly an' peaceable, an' we've 'poligized for hurtin' you; but if that don't satisfy you, you'll have to make the most of it. You may be the Boolooroo of the Blues, but you ain't even a tin whistle to us, an' you can't skeer us for half a minute. I'm an ol' man, myself, but if you don't behave I'll spank you like I would a baby, an' it won't be any trouble at all to do it, thank'e. As a matter o' fact, we've captured your whole bloomin' blue island, but we don't like the place very much, and I guess we'll give it back. It gives us the blues — don't it, Trot? — so as soon as we eat a bite o' lunch from our basket we'll sail away again."

"Sail away? How?" asked the Boolooroo.

"With the Magic Umbrel," said Cap'n Bill, pointing to the umbrella that Button-Bright was holding underneath his arm.

"Oh, ho! I see — I see," said the Boolooroo, nodding his funny head. "Go ahead, then, and eat your lunch."

He retreated a little way to a marble seat beside the fountain, but watched the strangers carefully. Cap'n Bill, feeling sure he had won the argument, whispered to the boy and girl that they must eat and get away as soon as possible, as this might prove a dangerous country for them to remain in. Trot longed to see more of the strange blue island, and especially wanted to explore the magnificent blue palace that adjoined the garden, and which had six hundred tall towers and turrets; but she felt that her old friend was wise in advising them to get away quickly. So she opened the basket and they all three sat in a row on a stone bench and began to eat sandwiches and cake and pickles and cheese and all the good things that were packed in the lunch basket.

They were hungry from the long ride, and while they ate they kept their eyes busily employed in examining all the queer things around them. The Boolooroo seemed quite the queerest of anything, and Trot noticed that when he pulled the long curl that stuck up from the top of his head a bell tinkled somewhere in the palace. He next pulled at the bottom of his right ear, and another far-away bell tinkled; then he touched the end of his nose and still another bell was faintly heard. The Boolooroo said not a word while he was ringing the bells, and Trot wondered if that was the way he amused himself. But now the frown died away from his face and was replaced by a look of satisfaction.

"Have you nearly finished?" he inquired.

"No," said Trot; "we've got to eat our apples yet."

"Apples — apples? What are apples?" he asked.

Trot took some from the basket.

"Have one?" she said. "They're awful good."

The Boolooroo advanced a step and took the apple, which he regarded with much curiosity.

"Guess they don't grow anywhere but on the Earth," remarked Cap'n Bill.

"Are they good to eat?" asked the Boolooroo.

"Try it and see," answered Trot, biting into an apple herself.

Chapter Five

The Blueskin sat down on the end of their bench, next to Button-Bright, and began to eat his apple. He seemed to like it, for he finished it in a hurry, and when it was gone he picked up the Magic Umbrella.

"Let that alone!" said Button-Bright, making a grab for it. But the Boolooroo jerked it away in an instant and standing up he held the umbrella behind him and laughed aloud.

"Now, then," said he, "you can't get away until I'm willing to let you go. You are my prisoners."

"I guess not," returned Cap'n Bill, and reaching out one of his long arms, the sailorman suddenly grasped the Boolooroo around his long, thin neck and shook him until his whole body fluttered like a flag.

"Drop that umbrel — drop it!" yelled Cap'n Bill, and the Boolooroo quickly obeyed. The Magic Umbrella fell to the ground and Button-Bright promptly seized it. Then the sailor let go his hold and the King staggered to a seat, choking and coughing to get his breath back.

"I told you to let things alone," growled Cap'n Bill. "If you don't behave, your Majesty, this Blue Island 'll have to get another Boolooroo."

"Why?" asked the Blueskin.

"Because I'll prob'ly spoil you for a king, an' mebbe for anything else. Anyhow, you'll get badly damaged if you try to interfere with us — an' that's a fact."

"Don't kill him, Cap'n Bill," said Trot, cheerfully.

61

"Kill me? Why, he couldn't do that," observed the King, who was trying to rearrange the ruffle around his neck. "Nothing can kill me."

"Why not?" asked Cap'n Bill.

"Because I haven't lived my six hundred years yet. Perhaps you don't know that every Blueskin in Sky Island lives exactly six hundred years from the time he is born."

"No; I didn't know that," admitted the sailor.

"It's a fact," said the King. "Nothing can kill us until we've lived to the last day of our appointed lives. When the final minute is up, we die; but we're obliged to live all of the six hundred years, whether we want to or not. So you needn't think of trying to kill anybody on Sky Island. It can't be done."

"Never mind," said Cap'n Bill. "I'm no murderer, thank goodness, and I wouldn't kill you if I could—much as you deserve it."

"But isn't six hundred years an awful long time to live?" questioned Trot.

"It seems like it, at first," replied the King, "but I notice that whenever any of my subjects get near the end of their six hundred, they grow nervous and say the life is altogether too short."

"How long have you lived?" asked Button-Bright.

The King coughed again and turned a bit bluer.

"That is considered an impertinent question in Sky

Island," he answered; "but I will say that every Boolooroo is elected to reign three hundred years, and I've reigned not quite — ahem! — two hundred."

"Are your kings elected, then?" asked Cap'n Bill.

"Yes, of course; this is a Republic, you know. The people elect all their officers, from the King down. Every man and every woman is a voter. The Boolooroo tells them whom to vote for, and if they don't obey they are severely punished. It's a fine system of government, and the only thing I object to is electing the Boolooroo for only three hundred years. It ought to be for life. My successor has already been elected, but he can't reign for a hundred years to come."

"I think three hundred years is plenty long enough," said Trot. "It gives some one else a chance to rule, an' I wouldn't be s'prised if the next king is a better one. Seems to me you're not much of a Boolooroo."

"That," replied the King, indignantly, "is a matter of opinion. I like myself very much, but I can't expect you to like me, because you're deformed and ignorant."

"I'm not!" cried Trot.

"Yes, you are. Your legs are too short and your neck is nothing at all. Your color is most peculiar, but there isn't a shade of blue about any of you, except the deep blue color of the clothes the old ape that choked me wears. Also, you are ignorant, because you know nothing of Sky Island, which is

63

the Center of the Universe and the only place anyone would care to live."

"Don't listen to him, Trot," said Button-Bright; "he's an ignorant himself."

Cap'n Bill packed up the lunch basket. One end of the rope was still tied to the handle of the basket and the other end to his swing seat, which lay on the ground before them.

"Well," said he, "let's go home. We've seen enough of this Blue Country and its Blue Boolooroo, I guess, an' it's a long journey back again."

"All right," agreed Trot, jumping up.

Button-Bright stood on the bench and held up the Magic Umbrella, so he could open it, and the sailor had just attached the ropes when a thin blue line shot out from behind them and in a twinkling wound itself around the umbrella. At the same instant another blue cord wound itself around the boy's body, and others caught Trot and Cap'n Bill in their coils, so that all had their arms pinned fast to their sides and found themselves absolutely helpless.

THE SIX SNUBNOSED PRINCESSES

CHAPTER 6.

THE Boolooroo was laughing and dancing around in front of them as if well pleased. For a moment the prisoners could not imagine what had happened to them, but presently half a dozen Blueskins, resembling in shape and costume their ruler but less magnificently dressed, stepped in front of them and bowed low to the Boolooroo.

"Your orders, most Mighty, Flighty, Tight and Righty Monarch, have been obeyed," said the leader.

"Very well, Captain. Take that umbrella and carry it to my Royal Treasury. See that it is safely locked up. Here's the key, and if you don't return it to me within five minutes I'll have you patched."

The Captain took the key and the Magic Umbrella and hastened away to the palace. Button-Bright had already hooked the ropes to the elephant-trunk handle, so that when the Captain carried away the umbrella he dragged after him

65

first the double seat, then Cap'n Bill's seat, which was fastened to it, and finally the lunch-basket, which was attached to the lower seat. At every few steps some of these would trip up the Captain and cause him to take a tumble, but as he had only five minutes' time in which to perform his errand he would scramble to his feet again and dash along the path until a board or the basket tripped him again.

They all watched him with interest until he had disappeared within the palace, when the King turned to his men and said:

"Release the prisoners. They are now quite safe, and cannot escape me."

So the men unwound the long cords that were twined around the bodies of our three friends, and set them free. These men seemed to be soldiers, although they bore no arms except the cords. Each cord had a weight at the end, and when the weight was skillfully thrown by a soldier it wound the cord around anything in the twinkling of an eye and held fast until it was unwound again.

Trot decided these Blueskins must have stolen into the garden when summoned by the bells the Boolooroo had rung, but they had kept out of sight and crept up behind the bench on which our friends were seated, until a signal from the king aroused them to action.

The little girl was greatly surprised by the suddenness of her capture, and so was Button-Bright. Cap'n Bill shook his head and said he was afeared they'd get into trouble. "Our mistake," he added, "was in stoppin' to eat our lunch. But it's too late now to cry over spilt milk."

"I don't mind; not much, anyhow," asserted Trot, bravely. "We're in no hurry to get back; are we, Button-Bright?"

"I'm not," said the boy. "If they hadn't taken the umbrella I wouldn't care how long we stopped in this funny island. Do you think it's a fairy country, Trot?"

"Can't say, I'm sure," she answered. "I haven't seen anything here yet that reminds me of fairies; but Cap'n Bill said a floating island in the sky was sure to be a fairyland."

"I think so yet, mate," returned the sailor. "But there's all sorts o' fairies, I've heard. Some is good, an' some is bad, an' if all the Blueskins are like their Boolooroo they can't be called fust-class."

"Don't let me hear any more impudence, prisoners!" called the Boolooroo, sternly. "You are already condemned to severe punishment, and if I have any further trouble with you, you are liable to be patched."

"What's being patched?" inquired the girl.

The soldiers all laughed at this question, but the King did not reply. Just then a door in the palace opened and out trooped a group of girls. There were six of them, all gorgeously dressed in silken gowns with many puffs and tucks and ruffles and flounces and laces and ribbons, everything being in some shade of blue, grading from light blue to deep blue. Their blue hair was elaborately dressed and came to a point at the top of their heads.

The girls approached in a line along the garden path, all walking with mincing steps and holding their chins high. Their skirts prevented their long legs from appearing as grotesque as did those of the men, but their necks were so thin and long that the ruffles around them only made them seem the more absurd.

"Ah," said the King, with a frown, "here come the Six Snubnosed Princesses — the most beautiful and aristocratic ladies in Sky Island."

"They're snubnosed, all right," observed Trot, looking at

the girls with much interest; "but I should think it would make 'em mad to call 'em that."

"Why?" asked the Boolooroo, in surprise. "Is not a snubnose the highest mark of female beauty?"

"Is it?" asked the girl.

"Most certainly. In this favored island, which is the Center of the Universe, a snubnose is an evidence of high breeding which any lady would be proud to possess."

The Six Snubnosed Princesses now approached the fountain and stood in a row, staring with haughty looks at the strangers.

"Goodness me, your Majesty!" exclaimed the first; "what queer, dreadful-looking creatures are these? Where in all the Sky did they come from?"

"They say they came from the Earth, Cerulia," answered the Boolooroo.

"But that is impossible," said another Princess. "Our scientists have proved that the Earth is not inhabited."

"Your scientists'll have to guess again, then," said Trot.

"But how did they get to Sky Island?" inquired the third snubnosed one.

"By means of a Magic Umbrella, which I have captured and put away in my Treasure Chamber," replied the Boolooroo.

"What will you do with the monsters, papa?" asked the fourth Princess.

"I haven't decided yet," said the Boolooroo. "They're curiosities, you see, and may serve to amuse us. But as they're only half civilized I shall make them my slaves."

"What are they good for? Can they do anything useful?" asked the fifth.

"We'll see," returned the King, impatiently. "I can't decide in a hurry. Give me time, Azure; give me time. If there's anything I hate it's a hurry."

"I've an idea, your Majesty," announced the sixth Snubnosed Princess, whose complexion was rather darker than that of her sisters, "and it has come to me quite deliberately, without any hurry at all. Let us take the little girl to be our maid —to wait upon us and amuse us when we're dull. All the other ladies of the court will be wild with envy, and if the child doesn't prove of use to us we can keep her for a living pincushion."

"Oh! Ah! That will be fine!" cried all the other five, and the Boolooroo said:

"Very well, Indigo; it shall be as you desire." Then he turned to Trot and added: "I present you to the Six Lovely Snubnosed Princesses, to be their slave. If you are good and obedient you won't get your ears boxed oftener than once an hour."

"I won't be anybody's slave," protested Trot. "I don't like these snubnosed, fussy females an' I won't have anything to do with 'em."

"How impudent!" cried Cerulia.

"How vulgar!" cried Turquoise.

"How unladylike!" cried Sapphire.

"How silly!" cried Azure.

"How absurd!" cried Cobalt.

"How wicked!" cried Indigo. And then all six held up their hands as if horrified.

The Boolooroo laughed.

"You'll know how to bring her to time, I imagine," he remarked, "and if the girl isn't reasonable and obedient, send her to me and I'll have her patched. Now, then, take her away."

But Trot was obstinate and wouldn't budge a step.

"Keep us together, your Majesty," begged Cap'n Bill. "If we're to be slaves, don't separate us, but make us all the same kind o' slaves."

"I shall do what pleases me," declared the Boolooroo, angrily. "Don't try to dictate, old Moonface, for there's only one Royal Will in Sky Island, and that's my own."

He then gave a command to a soldier, who hastened away to the palace and soon returned with a number of long blue ribbons. One he tied around Trot's waist and then attached to it six other ribbons. Each of the Six Snubnosed Princesses held the end of a ribbon, and then they turned and marched haughtily away to the palace, dragging the little girl after them.

"Don't worry, Trot," cried Button-Bright; "we'll get you out of this trouble pretty soon."

"Trust to us, mate," added Cap'n Bill; "we'll manage to take care o' you."

"Oh, I'm all right," answered Trot, with fine courage; "I'm not afraid of these gawkies."

But the princesses pulled her after them and soon they had all disappeared into one of the entrances to the Blue Palace.

"Now, then," said the Boolooroo, "I will instruct you two in your future duties. I shall make old Moonface—"

"My name's Cap'n Bill Weedles," interrupted the sailor.

"I don't care what your name is; I shall call you old Moonface," replied the king, "for that suits you quite well. I shall appoint you the Royal Nectar Mixer to the Court of

Sky Island, and if you don't mix our nectar properly I'll have you patched.

"How do you mix it?" asked Cap'n Bill.

"I don't mix it; it's **not the** Boolooroo's place to mix nectar," was the stern reply. "But you may inquire of the palace servants and perhaps the Royal Chef **or** the Major-domo will condescend to tell you. Take him to the servants' quarters, Captain Ultramarine, and give him a suit of the royal livery."

So Cap'n Bill was led away by the chief of the soldiers, **and** when he had gone the king said to Button-Bright:

"You, slave, shall be the Royal Bootblue. Your duty will be to keep the boots and shoes of the royal family nicely polished with blue."

"I don't know how," answered Button-Bright, surlily.

"You'll soon learn. The Royal Steward will supply you with blue paste, and when you've brushed this on our shoes you must shine them with Q-rays of Moonshine. Do you understand?"

"No," said Button-Bright.

Then the Boolooroo told one of the soldiers to take the boy to the shoeblue den and have him instructed in his duties, and the soldier promptly obeyed and dragged Button-Bright away to the end of the palace where the servants lived.

GHIP-GHISIZZLE PROVES FRIENDLY

CHAPTER 7.

THE Royal Palace was certainly a magnificent building, with large and lofty rooms and superb furnishings, all being in shades of blue. The soldier and the boy passed through several broad corridors and then came to a big hall where many servants were congregated. These were staring in bewilderment at Cap'n Bill, who had been introduced to them by Captain Ultramarine. Now they turned in no less surprise to examine the boy, and their looks expressed not only astonishment but dislike.

The servants were all richly attired in blue silk liveries and they seemed disposed to resent the fact that these strangers had been added to their ranks. They scowled and muttered and behaved in a very unfriendly way, even after Captain Ultramarine had explained that the newcomers were merely base slaves, and not to be classed with the free royal servants of the palace.

Chapter Seven

One of those present, however, showed no especial enmity to Button-Bright and Cap'n Bill, and this Blueskin attracted the boy's notice because his appearance was so strange. He looked as if he were made of two separate men, each cut through the middle and then joined together, half of one to half of the other. One side of his blue hair was curly and the other half straight; one ear was big and stuck out from the side of his head, while the other ear was small and flat; one eye was half shut and twinkling while the other was big and staring; his nose was thin on one side and flat on the other, while one side of his mouth curled up and the other down. Button-Bright also noticed that he limped as he walked, because one leg was a trifle longer than the other, and that one hand was delicate and slender and the other thick and hardened by use.

"Don't stare at him," a voice whispered in the boy's ear; "the poor fellow has been patched, that's all."

Button-Bright turned to see who had spoken and found by his side a tall young Blueskin with a blue-gold chain around his neck. He was quite the best looking person the boy had seen in Sky Island and he spoke in a pleasant way and seemed quite friendly. But the two-sided man had overheard the remark and he now stepped forward and said, in a careless tone:

"Never mind; it's no disgrace to be patched in a country ruled by such a cruel Boolooroo as we have. Let the boy look at me, if he wants to; I'm not pretty, but that's not my fault. Blame the Boolooroo."

"I—I'm glad to meet you, sir," stammered Button-Bright. "What is your name, please?"

"I'm now named Jimfred Jonesjinks, and my partner is called Fredjim Jinksjones. He's busy at present guarding the Treasure Chamber, but I'll introduce you to him when he comes back. We've had the misfortune to be patched, you know."

"What is being patched?" asked the boy.

"They cut two of us in halves and mismatch the halves — half of one to half of the other, you know — and then the other two halves are patched together. It destroys our individuality and makes us complex creatures, so it's the worst punishment than can be inflicted in Sky Island."

"Oh," said Button-Bright, alarmed at such dreadful butchery; "does n't it hurt?"

"No; it does n't hurt," replied Jimfred, "but it makes one frightfully nervous. They stand you under a big knife, which drops and slices you neatly in two — exactly in the middle. Then they match half of you to another person who has likewise been sliced — and there you are, patched to some-one you don't care about and have n't much interest in. If your half wants to do something, the other half is likely to want to do something different, and the funny part of it is you don't quite know which is your half and which is the

76

other half. It's a terrible punishment, and in a country where one can't die or be killed until he has lived his six hundred years, to be patched is a great misfortune."

"I'm sure it is," said Button-Bright, earnestly. "But can't you ever get — get — *un*-patched again?"

"If the Boolooroo would consent, I think it could be done," Jimfred replied; "but he never will consent. This is about the meanest Boolooroo who ever ruled this land, and he was the first to invent patching people as a punishment. I think we will all be glad when his three hundred years of rule are ended."

"When will that be?" inquired the boy.

"Hush-sh-sh!" cried everyone, in a chorus, and they all looked over their shoulders as if frightened by the question. The officer with the blue-gold chain pulled Button-Bright's sleeve and whispered:

"Follow me, please." And then he beckoned to Cap'n Bill and led the two slaves to another room, where they were alone.

"I must instruct you in your duties," said he, when they were all comfortably seated in cosy chairs with blue cushions. "You must learn how to obey the Boolooroo's commands, so he won't become angry and have you patched."

"How could he patch *us*?" asked the sailorman, curiously.

"Oh, he'd just slice you all in halves and then patch half of the boy to half of the girl, and the other half to half of you, and the other half of you to the other half of the girl. See?"

"Can't say I do," said Cap'n Bill, much bewildered. "It's a reg'lar mix-up."

"That's what it's meant to be," explained the young officer.

"An' seein' as we're Earth folks, an' not natives of Sky Island, I've an idea the slicing machine would about end us, without bein' patched," continued the sailor.

"Oh," said Button-Bright; "so it would."

"While you are in this country you can't die till you've lived six hundred years," declared the officer.

"Oh," said Button-Bright; "that's different, of course. But who are you, please?"

"My name is Ghip-Ghi-siz-zle. Can you remember it?"

"I can 'member the 'sizzle,'" said the boy; "but I'm 'fraid the Gwip—Grip—Glip——"

"Ghip-Ghi-siz-zle," repeated the officer, slowly. "I want you to remember my name, because if you are going to live here you are sure to hear of me a great many times. Can you keep a secret?"

"I can try," said Button-Bright.

"I've kep' secrets—once in a while," asserted Cap'n Bill.

"Well, try to keep this one. I'm to be the next Boolooroo of Sky Island."

"Good for you!" cried the sailor. "I wish you was the

Boolooroo now, sir. But it seems you've got to wait a hundred years or more afore you can take his place."

Ghip-Ghisizzle rose to his feet and paced up and down the room for a time, a frown upon his blue face. Then he halted and faced Cap'n Bill.

"Sir," said he, "there lies all my trouble. I'm quite sure the present Boolooroo has reigned three hundred years next Thursday; but he claims it is only two hundred years, and as he holds the Royal Book of Records under lock and key in the Royal Treasury, there is no way for us to prove he is wrong."

"Oh," said Button-Bright. "How old is the Boolooroo?"

"He was two hundred years old when he was elected," replied Ghip-Ghisizzle. "If he has already reigned three hundred years, as I suspect, then he is now five hundred years old. You see, he is trying to steal another hundred years of rule, so as to remain a tyrant all his life."

"He don't seem as old as that," observed Cap'n Bill, thoughtfully. "Why, I'm only sixty, myself, an' I guess I look twice as old as your king does."

"We do not show our age in looks," the officer answered. "I am just about your own age, sir—sixty-two my next birthday—but I'm sure I don't look as old as you."

"That's a fact," agreed Cap'n Bill. Then he turned to Button-Bright and added: "Don't that prove Sky Island is a fairy country, as I said?"

"Oh, I've known that all along," said the boy. "The

slicing and patching proves it, and so do lots of other things."

"Now, then," said Ghip-Ghisizzle, "let us talk over your duties. It seems you must mix the royal nectar, Cap'n Bill. Do you know how to do that?"

"I'm free to say as I don't, friend Sizzle."

"The Boolooroo is very particular about his nectar. I think he has given you this job so he can find fault with you and have you punished. But we will fool him. You are strangers here, and I don't want you imposed upon. I'll send Tiggle to the royal pantry and keep him there to mix the nectar. Then when the Boolooroo, or the Queen, or any of the Snubnosed Princesses call for a drink, you can carry it to them and it will be sure to suit them."

"Thank 'e, sir," said Cap'n Bill; "that's real kind of you."

"Your job, Button-Bright, is easier," continued Ghip-Ghisizzle.

"I'm no bootblack," declared the boy. "The Boolooroo has no right to make me do his dirty work."

"You're a slave," the officer reminded him, "and a slave must obey."

"Why?" asked Button-Bright.

"Because he can't help himself. No slave ever wants to obey, but he just has to. And it isn't dirty work at all. You don't black the royal boots and shoes; you merely blue them with a finely perfumed blue paste. Then you shine them neatly and your task is done. You will not be humiliated by becoming a bootblack. You'll be a bootblue."

"Oh," said Button-Bright. "I don't see much difference, but perhaps it's a little more respectable."

"Yes; the Royal Bootblue is considered a high official in Sky Island. You do your work at evening or early morning, and the rest of the day you are at liberty to do as you please."

"It won't last long, Button-Bright," said Cap'n Bill, consolingly. "Somethin's bound to happen pretty soon, you know."

"I think so myself," answered the boy.

"And now," remarked Ghip-Ghisizzle, "since you understand your new duties, perhaps you'd like to walk out with me and see the Blue City and the glorious Blue Country of Sky Island."

"We would that!" cried Cap'n Bill, promptly.

So they accompanied their new friend through a maze of passages—for the palace was very big—and then through a high arched portal into the streets of the City. So rapid had been their descent when the umbrella landed them in the royal garden that they had not even caught a glimpse of the Blue City, so now they gazed with wonder and interest at the splendid sights that met their eyes.

THE BLUE CITY

CHAPTER 8.

THE Blue City was quite extensive, and consisted of many broad streets paved with blue marble and lined with splendid buildings of the same beautiful material. There were houses and castles and shops for the merchants and all were prettily designed and had many slender spires and imposing turrets that rose far into the blue air. Everything was blue here, just as was everything in the Royal Palace and gardens, and a blue haze overhung all the city.

"Doesn't the sun ever shine?" asked Cap'n Bill.

"Not in the blue part of Sky Island," replied Ghip-Ghisizzle. "The moon shines here every night, but we never see the sun. I am told, however, that on the other half of the Island—which I have never seen—the sun shines brightly but there is no moon at all."

"Oh," said Button-Bright; "is there another half to Sky Island?"

"Yes; a dreadful place called the Pink Country. I'm told everything there is pink instead of blue. A fearful place it must be, indeed!" said the Blueskin, with a shudder.

"I dunno 'bout that," remarked Cap'n Bill. "That Pink Country sounds kind o' cheerful to me. Is your Blue Country very big?"

"It is immense," was the proud reply. "This enormous City extends a half mile in all directions from the center, and the country outside the City is fully a half mile further in extent. That's very big, isn't it?"

"Not very," replied Cap'n Bill, with a smile. "We've cities on the Earth ten times bigger—an' then some big besides. We'd call this a small town in our country."

"Our Country is thousands of miles wide and thousands

of miles long—it's the great United States of America!"
added the boy, earnestly.

Ghip-Ghisizzle seemed astonished. He was silent a moment, and then he said:

"Here in Sky Island we prize truthfulness very highly. Our Boolooroo is not very truthful, I admit, for he is trying to misrepresent the length of his reign, but our people as a rule speak only the truth."

"So do we," asserted Cap'n Bill. "What Button-Bright said is the honest truth—every word of it."

"But we have been led to believe that Sky Island is the greatest country in the universe—meaning, of course, our half of it, the Blue Country."

"It may be for you, perhaps," the sailor stated, politely, "an' I don't imagine any island floatin' in the sky is any bigger. But the Universe is a big place an' you can't be sure of what's in it till you've traveled, like we have."

"Perhaps you are right," mused the Blueskin; but he still seemed to doubt them.

"Is the Pink side of Sky Island bigger than the Blue side?" asked Button-Bright.

"No; it is supposed to be the same size," was the reply.

"Then why haven't you ever been there? Seems to me you could walk across the whole island in an hour," said the boy.

"The two parts are separated by an impassable barrier,"

answered Ghip-Ghisizzle. "Between them lies the Great Fog Bank."

"A fog bank? Why, that's no barrier!" exclaimed Cap'n Bill.

"It is, indeed," returned the Blueskin. "The Fog Bank is so thick and heavy that it blinds one, and if once you got into the Bank you might wander forever and not find your way out again. Also it is full of dampness that wets your clothes and your hair until you become miserable. It is furthermore said that those who enter the Fog Bank forfeit the six hundred years allowed them to live, and are liable to die at any time. Here we do not die, you know; we merely pass away."

"How's that?" asked the sailor. "Isn't 'pass'n' away' jus' the same as dyin'?"

"No, indeed. When our six hundred years are ended we march into the Great Blue Grotto, through the Arch of Phinis, and are never seen again."

"That's queer," said Button-Bright. "What would happen if you didn't march through the Arch?"

"I do not know, for no one has ever refused to do so. It is the Law, and we all obey it."

"It saves funeral expenses, anyhow," remarked Cap'n Bill. "Where is this Arch?"

"Just outside the gates of the City. There is a mountain in the center of the Blue land, and the entrance to the Great

Sky Island

Blue Grotto is at the foot of the mountain. According to our figures the Boolooroo ought to march into this Grotto a hundred years from next Thursday, but he is trying to steal a hundred years and so perhaps he won't enter the Arch of Phinis. Therefore, if you will please be patient for about a hundred years, you will discover what happens to one who breaks the Law."

"Thank'e," remarked Cap'n Bill. "I don't expect to be very curious, a hundred years from now."

"Nor I," added Button-Bright, laughing at the whimsical speech. "But I don't see how the Boolooroo is able to fool you all. Can't any of you remember two or three hundred years back, when he first began to rule?"

"No," said Ghip-Ghisizzle; "that's a long time to remember, and we Blueskins try to forget all we can—especially whatever is unpleasant. Those who remember are usually the unhappy ones; only those able to forget find the most joy in life."

During this conversation they had been walking along the streets of the Blue City, where many of the Blueskin inhabitants stopped to gaze wonderingly at the sailor and the boy, whose strange appearance surprised them. They were a nervous, restless people and their egg-shaped heads, set on the ends of long thin necks, seemed so grotesque to the strangers that they could scarcely forbear laughing at them. The bodies of these people were short and round and their legs

86

exceptionally long, so when a Blueskin walked he covered twice as much ground at one step as Cap'n Bill or Button-Bright did. The women seemed just as repellent as the men, and Button-Bright began to understand that the Six Snub-nosed Princesses were, after all, rather better looking than most of the females of the Blue Country and so had a certain right to be proud and haughty.

There were no horses nor cows in this land, but there were plenty of blue goats, from which the people got their milk. Children tended the goats—wee Blueskin boys and girls whose appearance was so comical that Button-Bright laughed whenever he saw one of them.

Although the natives had never seen before this any human beings made as Button-Bright and Cap'n Bill were, they took a strong dislike to the strangers and several times threatened to attack them. Perhaps if Ghip-Ghisizzle, who was their favorite, had not been present, they would have mobbed our friends with vicious ill-will and might have seriously injured them. But Ghip-Ghisizzle's friendly protection made them hold aloof.

By and by they passed through a City gate and their guide showed them the outer walls, which protected the City from the country beyond. There were several of these gates, and from their recesses stone steps led to the top of the wall. They mounted a flight of these steps and from their elevation plainly saw the low mountain where the Arch of Phinis was located, and beyond that the thick, blue-gray Fog Bank, which constantly rolled like billows of the ocean and really seemed, from a distance, quite forbidding.

"But it wouldn't take long to get there," decided Button-Bright, "and if you were close up it might not be worse than any other fog. Is the Pink Country on the other side of it?"

"So we are told in the Book of Records," replied Ghip-Ghisizzle. "None of us now living know anything about it, but the Book of Records calls it the 'Sunset Country,' and says that at evening the pink shades are drowned by terrible colors of orange and crimson and golden-yellow and red. Wouldn't it be horrible to be obliged to look upon such a sight? It must give the poor people who live there dreadful headaches."

"I'd like to see that Book of Records," mused Cap'n Bill, who didn't think the discription of the Sunset Country at all dreadful.

"I'd like to see it myself," returned Ghip-Ghisizzle, with a sigh; "but no one can lay hands on it because the Boolooroo keeps it safely locked up in his Treasure Chamber."

"Where's the key to the Treasure Chamber?" asked Button-Bright.

"The Boolooroo keeps it in his pocket, night and day," was the reply. "He is afraid to let anyone see the Book, because it would prove he has already reigned three hundred years next Thursday, and then he would have to resign the throne to me and leave the Palace and live in a common house."

"My Magic Umbrella is in that Treasure Chamber," said Button-Bright, "and I'm going to try to get it."

"Are you?" inquired Ghip-Ghisizzle, eagerly. "Well, if you manage to enter the Treasure Chamber, be sure to bring me the Book of Records. If you can do that I will be the best and most grateful friend you ever had!"

"I'll see," said the boy. "It ought not to be hard work to break into the Treasure Chamber. Is it guarded?"

"Yes; the outside guard is Jimfred Jinksjones, the double patch of the Fredjim whom you have met, and the inside guard is a ravenous creature known as the Blue Wolf, which has teeth a foot long and as sharp as needles."

"Oh," said Button-Bright. "But never mind the Blue Wolf; I must manage to get my umbrella, somehow or other."

They now walked back to the palace, still objects of much curiosity to the natives, who sneered at them and mocked them but dared not interfere with their progress. At the palace they found that dinner was about to be served in the big dining hall of the servants and dependents and household officers of the royal Boolooroo. Ghip-Ghisizzle was the Majordomo and Master of Ceremonies, so he took his seat at the end of the long table and placed Cap'n Bill on one side of him and Button-Bright on the other, to the great annoyance of the other Blueskins present, who favored the strangers with nothing pleasanter than envious scowls.

The Boolooroo and his Queen and daughters — the Six Snubnosed Princesses — dined in formal state in the Banquet Hall, where they were waited upon by favorite soldiers of the Royal Bodyguard. Here in the servants' hall there was one vacant seat next to Button-Bright which was reserved for Trot; but the little girl had not yet appeared and the sailorman and the boy were beginning to be uneasy about her.

THE TRIBULATION OF TROT

CHAPTER 9.

THE apartments occupied by the Six Snubnosed Princesses were so magnificent that when Trot first entered them, led by her haughty captors, she thought they must be the most beautiful rooms in all the world. There was a long and broad reception room, with forty-seven windows in it, and opening out of it were six lovely bedchambers, each furnished in the greatest luxury. Adjoining each sleeping room was a marble bath, and each Princess had a separate boudoir and a dressing room. The furnishings were of the utmost splendor, blue-gold and blue gems being profusely used in the decorations, while the divans and chairs were of richly carved bluewood upholstered in blue satins and silks. The draperies were superbly embroidered and the rugs upon the marble floors were woven with beautiful scenes in every conceivable shade of blue.

When they first reached the reception room Princess Azure cast herself upon a divan while her five sisters sat or reclined in easy chairs, with their heads thrown back and their blue chins scornfully elevated. Trot, who was much annoyed at the treatment she had received, did not hesitate to seat herself, also, in a big easy chair.

"Slave!" cried Princess Cerulia, "fetch me a mirror."

"Slave!" cried Princess Turquoise, "a lock of my hair is loosened; bind it up."

"Slave!" cried Princess Cobalt, "unfasten my shoes; they're too tight."

"Slave!" cried Princess Sapphire, "bring hither my box of blue chocolates."

"Slave!" cried Princess Azure, "stand by my side and fan me."

"Slave!" cried Princess Indigo, "get out of that chair. How dare you sit in our presence!"

"If you're saying all those things to me," replied Trot, "you may as well save your breath. I'm no slave." And she cuddled down closer in the chair.

"You *are* a slave!" shouted the six, all together.

"I'm not!"

"Our father, the Revered and Resplendent Royal Ruler of the Blues, has made you our slave," asserted Indigo, with a yawn.

"But he can't," objected the little girl. "I'm some Royal

an' Rapturous an' Ridic'lous myself, an' I won't allow any cheap Boolooroo to order me 'round."

"Are you of royal birth?" asked Azure, seeming surprised.

"Royal! Why, I'm an American, Snubnoses, and if there's anything royaler than an American I'd like to know what it is."

The Princesses seemed uncertain what reply to make to this speech and began whispering together. Finally Indigo said to Trot:

"We do not think it matters what you were in your own country, for having left there you have forfeited your rank. By recklessly intruding into our domain you have become a slave, and being a slave you must obey us or suffer the consequences."

"What cons'quences?" asked the girl.

"Dare to disobey us and you will quickly find out," snapped Indigo, swaying her head from side to side on its long, swan-like neck, like the pendulum of a clock.

"I don't want any trouble," said Trot, gravely. "We came to Sky Island by mistake, and wanted to go right away again; but your father wouldn't let us. It isn't our fault we're still here, an' I'm free to say you're a very dis'gree'ble an' horrid lot of people, with no manners to speak of, or you'd treat us nicely."

"No impertinence!" cried Indigo, savagely.

"Why, it's the truth," replied Trot.

Sky Island

Indigo made a rush and caught Trot by both shoulders. The Princess was twice the little girl's size and she shook her victim so violently that Trot's teeth rattled together. Then Princess Cobalt came up and slapped one side of the slave's face and Princess Turquoise ran forward and slapped the other side. Cerulia gave Trot a push one way and Sapphire pushed her the other way, so the little girl was quite out of breath and very angry when finally her punishment ceased. She had not been much hurt, though, and she was wise enough to understand that these Princesses were all cruel and vindictive, so that her safest plan was to pretend to obey them.

"Now, then," commanded Princess Indigo, "go and feed my little blue dog that crows like a rooster."

"And feed my pretty blue cat that sings like a bird," said Princess Azure.

"And feed my soft blue lamb that chatters like a monkey," said Princess Cobalt.

"And feed my poetic blue parrot that barks like a dog," said Princess Sapphire.

"And feed my fuzzy blue rabbit that roars like a lion," said Princess Turquoise.

"And feed my lovely blue peacock that mews like a cat," said Princess Cerulia.

"Anything else?" asked Trot, drawing a long breath.

"Not until you have properly fed our pets," replied Azure, with a scowl.

Chapter Nine

"What do they eat, then?"

"Meat!"

"Milk!"

"Clover!"

"Seeds!"

"Bread!"

"Carrots!"

"All right," said Trot; "where do you keep the menagerie?"

"Our pets are in our boudoirs," said Indigo, harshly. "What a little fool you are!"

"Perhaps," said Trot, pausing as she was about to leave the room, "when I grow up I'll be as big a fool as any of you."

Then she ran away to escape another shaking, and in the first boudoir she found the little blue dog curled up on a blue cushion in a corner. Trot patted his head gently and this surprised the dog, who was accustomed to cuffs and kicks. So he licked Trot's hand and wagged his funny little tail and then straightened up and crowed like a rooster. The girl was delighted with the queer doggie and she found some meat in a cupboard and fed him out of her hand, patting the tiny creature and stroking his soft blue hair. The doggie had never in his life known anyone so kind and gentle, so when Trot went into the next boudoir the animal followed close at her heels, wagging his tail every minute.

The blue cat was asleep on a window seat, but it woke up when Trot tenderly took it in her lap and fed it milk from a blue-gold dish. It was a pretty cat and instantly knew the little girl was a friend — vastly different from its own bad-tempered mistress — so it sang beautifully, as a bird sings, and both the cat and the dog followed Trot into the third boudoir.

Here was a tiny baby lamb with fleece as blue as a larkspur and as soft as silk.

"Oh, you darling!" cried Trot, hugging the little lamb tight in her arms. At once the lamb began chattering, just as a monkey chatters, only in the most friendly and grateful way, and Trot fed it a handful of fresh blue clover and smoothed and petted it until the lamb was eager to follow her wherever she might go.

When she came to the fourth boudoir a handsome blue parrot sat on a blue perch and began barking as if it were nearly starved. Then it cried out:

"Rub-a-dub, dub,—
Gimme some grub!"

Trot laughed and gave it some seeds, and while the parrot ate them she stroked gently his soft feathers. The bird seemed much astonished at the unusual caress, and turned upon the girl first one little eye and then the other, as if trying to discover why she was so kind. He had never experienced kind treatment in all his life. So it was no wonder

96

that when the little girl entered the fifth boudoir she was followed by the parrot, the lamb, the cat and the dog, who all stood beside her and watched her feed the peacock, which she found strutting around and mewing like a cat for his dinner. Said the parrot:

"I spy a peacock's eye
On every feather— I wonder why?"

The peacock soon came to love Trot as much as the other bird and all the beasts did, and it spread its tail and strutted after her into the next boudoir—the sixth one. As she entered this room Trot gave a start of fear, for a terrible roar, like the roar of a lion, greeted her. But there was no lion there; a fuzzy blue rabbit was making all the noise.

"For goodness sake, keep quiet," said Trot. "Here's a nice blue carrot for you. The color seems all wrong, but it may taste jus' as good as if it was red."

Evidently it did taste good, for the rabbit ate it greedily. When it was not roaring the creature was so soft and fluffy that Trot played with it and fondled it a long time after it had finished eating, and the rabbit played with the cat and the dog and the lamb and did not seem a bit afraid of the parrot or the peacock. But, all of a sudden, in pounced Princess Indigo, with a yell of anger.

"So, this is how you waste your time, is it?" exclaimed the Princess, and grabbing Trot's arm she jerked the girl to her feet and began pushing her from the room. All the pets began to follow her, and seeing this, Indigo yelled at them to keep back. As they paid no attention to this command the princess seized a basin of water and dashed the fluid over the beasts and birds, after which she renewed her attempt to push Trot from the room. The pets rebelled at such treatment, and believing they ought to protect Trot, whom they knew to be their friend, they proceeded to defend her. The little blue dog dashed at Indigo and bit her right ankle, while the blue cat scratched her left leg with its claws and the parrot flew upon her shoulder and pecked her ear. The lamb ran up and butted Indigo so that she stumbled forward on her face, when the peacock proceeded to pound her head with his wings. Indigo, screaming with fright, sprang to her feet again, but the rabbit ran between her legs and tripped her up, all the time roaring loudly like a lion, and the dog crowed triumphantly, as a rooster crows, while the cat warbled noisily and the lamb chattered and the parrot barked and the peacock screeched: "me-ow!"

Altogether, Indigo was, as Trot said, "scared stiff," and she howled for help until her sisters ran in and rescued her, pulling her through the bedchamber into the reception room.

When she was alone Trot sat down on the floor and laughed until the tears came to her eyes, and she hugged all the pets and kissed them every one and thanked them for protecting her.

Chapter Nine

"That's all right;
We like a fight,"

declared the parrot, in reply.

The Princesses were horrified to find Indigo so scratched and bitten, and they were likewise amazed at the rebellion of their six pets, which they had never petted, indeed, but kept in their boudoirs so they could abuse them whenever they felt especially wicked or ill-natured. None of the snubnosed ones dared enter the room where the girl was, but they called through a crack in the door for Trot to come out instantly. Trot, pretending not to hear, paid no attention to these commands.

Finding themselves helpless and balked of their revenge, the Six Snubnosed Princesses finally recovered from their excitement and settled down to a pleasant sisterly quarrel, as was their customary amusement. Indigo wanted to have Trot patched, and Cerulia wanted her beaten with knotted cords, and Cobalt wanted her locked up in a dark room, and Sapphire wanted her fed on sand, and Turquoise wanted her bound to a windmill, and so between these various desires they quarrelled and argued until dinner time arrived.

Trot was occupying Indigo's room, so that Princess was obliged to dress with Azure, not daring to enter her own chamber, and the two sisters quarrelled so enthusiastically that they almost came to blows before they were ready for dinner.

Before the Six Snubnosed Princesses went to the Royal

Sky Island

Banquet Hall, Cobalt stuck her head through a crack of the door and said to Trot:

"If you want any dinner, you'll find it in the servants' hall. I advise you to eat, for after our dinner we will decide upon a fitting punishment for you, and then I'm sure you won't have much appetite."

"Thank you," replied the girl; "I'm right hungry, jus' now."

She waited until the snubnosed sextette had pranced haughtily away and then she came out, followed by all the pets, and found her way to the servants' quarters.

THE KING'S TREASURE CHAMBER

CHAPTER 10.

ALL the Blueskins assembled in the servants' hall were amazed to see the pets of the Princesses trailing after the strange little girl, but Trot took her place next to Button-Bright at the table, and the parrot perched upon her shoulder, while the peacock stood upon one side of her chair, and the lamb upon the other, and the cat and dog lay at her feet, and the blue rabbit climbed into her lap and cuddled down there. Some of the Blueskins insisted that the animals and birds must be put out of the room, but Ghip-Ghisizzle said they could remain, as they were the favored pets of the lovely Snubnosed Princesses.

Cap'n Bill was delighted to see his dear little friend again, and so was Button-Bright, and now that they were reunited — for a time, at least — they paid little heed to the sour looks and taunting remarks of the ugly Blueskins and ate heartily of the dinner, which was really very good.

Sky Island

The meal was no sooner over than Ghip-Ghisizzle was summoned to the chamber of his Majesty the Boolooroo, but before he went away he took Trot and Cap'n Bill and Button-Bright into a small room and advised them to stay there until he returned, so that the servants and soldiers would not molest them.

"My people seem to dislike strangers," said the Majordomo, thoughtfully, "and that surprises me because you are the first strangers they have ever seen. I think they imagine you will become favorites of the Boolooroo and of the Princesses, and that is why they are jealous and hate you."

"They needn't worry 'bout that," replied Trot; "the Snubnoses hate me worse than the people do."

"I can't imagine a bootblue becoming a royal favorite," grumbled Button-Bright.

"Or a necktie mixer," added Cap'n Bill.

"You don't mix neckties; you're a nectar mixer," said Ghip-Ghisizzle, correcting the sailor. "I'll not be gone long, for I'm no favorite of the Boolooroo, either, so please stay quietly in this room until my return."

The Majordomo found the Boolooroo in a bad temper. He had finished his dinner, where his six daughters had bitterly denounced Trot all through the meal and implored their father to invent some new and terrible punishment for her. Also his wife, the Queen, had made him angry by begging for gold to buy ribbons with. Then, when he had retired to

Chapter Ten

his own private room, he decided to send for the umbrella he had stolen from Button-Bright, and test its magic powers. But the umbrella, in his hands, proved just as common as any other umbrella might. He opened it and closed it, and turned it this way and that, commanding it to do all sorts of things; but of course the Magic Umbrella would obey no one but a member of the family that rightfully owned it. At last the Boolooroo threw it down and stamped upon it and then kicked it into a corner, where it rolled underneath a cabinet. Then he sent for Ghip-Ghisizzle.

"Do you know how to work that Magic Umbrella?" he asked the Majordomo.

"No, your Majesty; I do not," was the reply.

"Well, find out. Make the Whiteskins tell you, so that I can use it for my own amusement."

"I'll do my best, your Majesty," said Ghip-Ghisizzle.

"You'll do more than that, or I'll have you patched!" roared the angry Boolooroo. "And don't waste any time, either, for as soon as we find out the secret of the umbrella I'm going to have the three strangers marched through the Arch of Phinis — and that will be the end of them."

"You can't do that, your Majesty," said the Majordomo.

"Why can't I?"

"They haven't lived six hundred years yet, and only those who have lived that length of time are allowed to march through the Arch of Phinis into the Great Blue Grotto."

The King looked at him with a sneer.

"Has anyone ever come out of that Arch alive?" he asked.

"No," said Ghip-Ghisizzle. "But no one has ever gone into the Blue Grotto until his allotted time was up."

"Well, I'm going to try the experiment," declared the Boolooroo. "I shall march these three strangers through the Arch, and if by any chance they come out alive I'll do a new sort of patching—I'll chop off their heads and mix 'em up, putting the wrong head on each of 'em. Ha, ha! Won't it be funny to see the old Moonface's head on the little girl? Ho, Ho! I really hope they'll come out of the Great Blue Grotto alive!"

"I also hope they will," replied Ghip-Ghisizzle.

"Then I'll bet you four button-holes they don't. I've a suspicion that once they enter the Great Blue Grotto that's the last of them."

Ghip-Ghisizzle went away quite sad and unhappy. He did not approve the way the strangers were being treated and thought it was wicked and cruel to try to destroy them.

During h'' absence the prisoners had been talking together very earnestly.

"We must get away from here, somehow 'r other," said Cap'n Bill; "but o' course we can't stir a step without the Magic Umbrel."

"No; I must surely manage to get my umbrella first," said Button-Bright.

"Do it quick, then," urged Trot, "for I can't stand those snubnoses much longer."

"I'll do it to-night," said the boy.

"The sooner the better, my lad," remarked the sailor; "but seein' as the Blue Boolooroo has locked it up in his Treasure Chamber, it may n't be easy to get hold of."

"No; it won't be easy," Button-Bright admitted. "But it has to be done, Cap'n Bill, and there's no use waiting any longer. No one here likes us, and in a few days they may make an end of us."

"Oh, Button-Bright! There's a Blue Wolf in the Treasure Chamber!" exclaimed Trot.

"Yes; I know."

"An' a patched man on guard outside," Cap'n Bill reminded him.

"I know," repeated Button-Bright.

"And the key's in the King's own pocket," added Trot, despairingly.

The boy nodded. He did n't say how he would overcome all these difficulties, so the little girl feared they would never see the Magic Umbrella again. But their present position was a very serious one and even Cap'n Bill dared not advise Button-Bright to give up the desperate attempt.

When Ghip-Ghisizzle returned he said:

"You must be very careful not to anger the Boolooroo, or he may do you a mischief. I think the little girl had better keep away from the Princesses for to-night, unless they demand her presence. The boy must go for the King's shoes and blue them and polish them and then take them back to the Royal Bedchamber. Cap'n Bill won't have anything to do, for I've ordered Tiggle to mix the nectar."

"Thank 'e, friend Sizzle," said Cap'n Bill.

"Now follow me and I will take you to your rooms."

He led them to the rear of the palace, where he gave them three small rooms on the ground floor, each having a bed in it. Cap'n Bill's room had a small door leading out into the street of the City, but Ghip-Ghisizzle advised him to keep this door locked, as the city people would be sure to hurt the strangers if they had the chance to attack them.

"You're safer in the palace than anywhere else," said the Majordomo, "for there is no way you can escape from the island, and here the servants and soldiers dare not injure you for fear of the Boolooroo."

He placed Trot and her six pets—which followed her wherever she went—in one room, and Cap'n Bill in another, and took Button-Bright away with him to show the boy the way to the King's bedchamber. As they proceeded they passed many rooms with closed doors, and before one of these a patched Blueskin was pacing up and down in a tired and sleepy way. It was Jimfred Jinksjones, the double of the

106

Chapter Ten

Fredjim Jonesjinks they had talked with in the servants' hall, and he bowed low before the Majordomo.

"This is the King's new bootblue, a stranger who has lately arrived here," said Ghip-Ghisizzle, introducing the boy to the patched man.

"I'm sorry for him," muttered Jimfred. "He's a queer looking chap, with his pale yellow skin, and I imagine our cruel Boolooroo is likely to patch him before long, as he did me — I mean us."

"No, he won't," said Button-Bright, positively. "The Boolooroo's afraid of me."

"Oh, that's different," said Jimfred. "You're the first person I ever knew that could scare our Boolooroo."

They passed on, and Ghip-Ghisizzle whispered: "That is the Royal Treasure Chamber."

Button-Bright nodded. He had marked the place well, so he couldn't miss it when he wanted to find it again.

When they came to the King's apartments there was another guard before the door, this time a long-necked soldier with a terrible scowl.

"This slave is the Royal Bootblue," said Ghip-Ghisizzle to the guard. "You will allow him to pass into his Majesty's chamber to get the royal shoes and to return them when they are blued."

"All right," answered the guard. "Our Boolooroo is in

an ugly mood to-night. It will go hard with this little short-necked creature if he does n't polish the shoes properly."

Then Ghip-Ghisizzle left Button-Bright and went away, and the boy passed through several rooms to the Royal Bed-chamber, where his Majesty sat undressing.

"Hi, there! What are you doing here?" he roared, as he saw Button-Bright.

"I've come for the shoes," said the boy.

The king threw them at his head, aiming carefully, but Button-Bright dodged the missiles and one smashed a mirror while the other shattered a vase on a small table. His Majesty looked around for something else to throw, but the boy seized the shoes and ran away, returning to his own room.

While he polished the shoes he told his plans to Cap'n Bill and Trot, and asked them to be ready to fly with him as soon as he returned with the Magic Umbrella. All they need to do was to step out into the street, through the door of Cap'n Bill's room, and open the umbrella. Fortunately, the seats and the lunch-basket were still attached to the handle — or so they thought — and there would be nothing to prevent their quickly starting on the journey home.

They waited a long time, however, to give the Boolooroo time to get to sleep, so it was after midnight when Button-Bright finally took the shoes in his hand and started for the Royal Bedchamber. He passed the guard of the Royal Treasury and Fredjim nodded good-naturedly to the boy. But the

Chapter Ten

sleepy guard before the King's apartments was cross and surly.

"What are you doing here at this hour?" he demanded.

"I'm returning his Majesty's shoes," said Button-Bright.

"Go back and wait till morning," commanded the guard.

"If you prevent me from obeying the Boolooroo's orders," returned the boy, quietly, "he will probably have you patched."

This threat frightened the long-necked guard, who did not know what orders the Boolooroo had given his Royal Boot-blue.

"Go in, then," said he; "but if you make a noise and waken his Majesty, the chances are you'll get yourself patched."

"I'll be quiet," promised the boy.

Indeed, Button-Bright had no desire to waken the Boolooroo, whom he found snoring lustily with the curtains of his high-posted bed drawn tightly around him. The boy had taken off his own shoes after he passed the guard and now he tiptoed carefully into the room, set down the royal shoes very gently and then crept to the chair where his Majesty's clothes were piled. Scarcely daring to breathe, for fear of awakening the terrible monarch, the boy searched in the royal pockets until he found a blue-gold key attached to a blue-gold chain. At once he decided this must be the key to the Treasure Cham-

109

ber, but in order to make sure he searched in every other pocket—without finding another key.

Then Button-Bright crept softly out of the room again, and in one of the outer rooms he sat down near a big cabinet and put on his shoes. Poor Button-Bright did not know that lying disregarded beneath that very cabinet at his side was the precious umbrella he was seeking, or that he was undertaking a desperate adventure all for nothing. He passed the long-necked guard again, finding the man half asleep, and then made his way to the Treasure Chamber. Facing Jimfred he said to the patched man, in a serious tone:

"His Majesty commands you to go at once to the corridor leading to the apartments of the Six Snubnosed Princesses and to guard the entrance until morning. You are to permit no one to enter or to leave the apartments."

"But—good gracious!" exclaimed the surprised Jimfred; "who will guard the Treasure Chamber?"

"I am to take your place," said Button-Bright.

"Oh, very well," replied Jimfred; "this is a queer freak for our Boolooroo to indulge in, but he is always doing something absurd. You're not much of a guard, seems to me, but if anyone tries to rob the Treasure Chamber you must ring this big gong, which will alarm the whole palace and bring the soldiers to your assistance. Do you understand?"

"Yes," said Button-Bright.

Then Fredjim stalked away to the other side of the palace

to guard the Princesses, and Button-Bright was left alone with the key to the Treasure Chamber in his hand. But he had not forgotten that the ferocious Blue Wolf was guarding the interior of the Chamber, so he searched in some of the rooms until he found a sofa-pillow, which he put under his arm and then returned to the corridor.

He placed the key in the lock and the bolt turned with a sharp click. Button-Bright did not hesitate. He was afraid, to be sure, and his heart was beating fast with the excitement of the moment, but he knew he must regain the Magic Umbrella if he would save his comrades and himself from destruction, for without it they could never return to the Earth. So he summoned up his best courage, opened the door, stepped quickly inside—and closed the door after him.

BUTTON-BRIGHT ENCOUNTERS THE BLUE WOLF

CHAPTER 11

A LOW, fierce growl greeted him. The Treasure Chamber was pretty dark, although the moonlight came in through some of the windows, but the boy had brought with him the low brass lamp that lighted the corridor and this he set upon a table beside the door before he took time to look around him.

The Treasure Chamber was heaped and crowded with all the riches the Boolooroo had accumulated during his reign of two or three hundred years. Piles of gold and jewels were on all sides and precious ornaments and splendid cloths, rare pieces of carved furniture, vases, bric-a-brac and the like, were strewn about the room in astonishing profusion.

Just at the boy's feet crouched a monstrous animal of most fearful aspect. He knew at a glance it was the terrible Blue Wolf and the sight of the beast sent a shiver through him. The Blue Wolf's head was fully as big as that of a lion and its wide jaws were armed with rows of long, pointed teeth. Its

112

shoulders and front legs were huge and powerful, but the rest of the wolf's body dwindled away until at the tail it was no bigger than a dog. The jaws were therefore the dangerous part of the creature, and its small blue eyes flashed wickedly at the intruder.

Just as the boy made his first step forward the Blue Wolf sprang upon him with its enormous jaws stretched wide open. Button-Bright jammed the sofa-pillow into the brute's mouth and crowded it in as hard as he could. The terrible teeth came together and buried themselves in the pillow, and then Mr. Wolf found he could not pull them out again — because his mouth was stuffed full. He could not even growl or yelp, but rolled upon the floor trying in vain to release himself from the conquering pillow.

Button-Bright paid no further attention to the helpless animal but caught up the blue-brass lamp and began a search for his umbrella. Of course he could not find it, as it was not there. He came across a small book, bound in light blue leather, which lay upon an exquisitely carved center-table. It was named, in dark blue letters stamped on the leather, "The Royal Record Book," and remembering that Ghip-Ghisizzle longed to possess this book Button-Bright hastily concealed it inside his blouse. Then he renewed his search for the umbrella, but it was quite in vain. He hunted in every crack and corner, tumbling the treasures here and there in the quest, but at last he became positive that the Magic Umbrella had been removed from the room.

The boy was bitterly disappointed and did not know what to do next. But he noticed that the Blue Wolf had finally seized an edge of the sofa-pillow in its sharp claws and was struggling to pull the thing out of his mouth; so, there being no object in his remaining longer in the room, where he might have to fight the wolf again, Button-Bright went out and locked the door behind him.

While he stood in the corridor wondering what to do next a sudden shouting reached his ears. It was the voice of the Boolooroo, crying: "My Key—my Key! Who has stolen my golden Key?" And then there followed shouts of soldiers and guards and servants and the rapid pattering of feet was heard throughout the palace.

Button-Bright took to his heels and ran along the passages until he came to Cap'n Bill's room, where the sailorman and Trot were anxiously awaiting him.

"Quick!" cried the boy; "we must escape from here at once or we will be caught and patched."

"Where's the umbrel?" asked Cap'n Bill.

"I don't know. I can't find it. But all the palace is aroused and the Boolooroo is furious. Come, let's get away at once!"

"Where'll we go?" inquired Trot

Chapter Eleven

"We must make for the open country and hide in the Fog Bank, or in the Arch of Phinis," replied the boy.

They did not stop to argue any longer, but all three stepped out of the little door into the street, where they first clasped hands, so they would not get separated in the dark, and then ran as swiftly as they could down the street, which was deserted at this hour by the citizens. They could not go very fast because the sailorman's wooden leg was awkward to run with and held them back, but Cap'n Bill hobbled quicker than he had ever hobbled before in all his life, and they really made pretty good progress.

They met no one on the streets and continued their flight until at last they came to the City Wall, which had a blue-iron gate in it. Here was a Blueskin guard, who had been peacefully slumbering when aroused by the footsteps of the fugitives.

"Halt!" cried the guard, fiercely.

Cap'n Bill halted long enough to grab the man around his long neck with one hand and around his long leg with the other hand. Then he raised the Blueskin in the air and threw him far over the wall. A moment later they had unfastened the gate and fled into the open country, where they headed toward the low mountain whose outlines were plainly visible in the moonlight.

The guard was now howling and crying for help. In the

city were answering shouts. A hue and cry came from every direction, reaching as far as the palace. Lights began to twinkle everywhere in the streets and the Blue City hummed like a beehive filled with angry bees.

"It won't do for us to get caught now," panted Cap'n Bill, as they ran along. "I'm more afeared o' them Blue citizens ner I am o' the Blue Boolooroo. They'd tear us to pieces, if they could."

Sky Island was not a very big place, especially the blue part of it, and our friends were now very close to the low mountain. Presently they paused before a grim archway of blue marble, above which was carved the one word: "Phinis." The interior seemed dark and terrible as they stopped to regard it as a possible place of refuge.

"Don't like that place, Cap'n," whispered Trot.

"No more do I, mate," he answered.

"I think I'd rather take a chance on the Fog Bank," said Button-Bright.

Just then they were all startled by a swift flapping of wings, and a voice cried in shrill tones:

"Where are you, Trot?
As like as not
I've been forgot!"

Cap'n Bill jumped this way and Button-Bright that, and

then there alighted on Trot's shoulder the blue parrot that had been the pet of the Princess Cerulia.

Said the bird:

> "Gee! I've flown
> Here all alone.
> It's pretty far,
> But here we are!"

and then he barked like a dog and chuckled with glee at having found his little friend.

In escaping from the palace Trot had been obliged to leave all the pets behind her, but it seemed that the parrot had found some way to get free and follow her. They were all astonished to hear the bird talk—and in poetry, too—but Cap'n Bill told Trot that some parrots he had known had possessed a pretty fair gift of language, and he added that this blue one seemed an unusually bright bird.

"As fer po'try," said he, "that's as how you look at po'try. Rhymes come from your head, but real po'try from your heart, an' whether the blue parrot has a heart or not he's sure got a head."

Having decided not to venture into the Arch of Phinis they again started on, this time across the country straight toward the Fog Bank, which hung like a blue-gray cloud directly across the center of the island. They knew they were being followed by bands of the Blueskins, for they could hear the shouts of their pursuers growing louder and louder every minute, since their long legs covered the ground more quickly than our friends could possibly go. Had the journey been much farther the fugitives would have been overtaken, but when the leaders of the pursuing Blueskins were only a few yards behind them they reached the edge of the Fog Bank and without hesitation plunged into its thick mist, which instantly hid them from view.

The Blueskins fell back, horrified at the mad act of the strangers. To them the Fog Bank was the most dreadful thing in existence and no Blueskin had ever ventured within it, even for a moment.

"That's the end of those short-necked Yellowskins," said one, shaking his head. "We may as well go back and report the matter to the Boolooroo."

THROUGH THE FOG BANK

CHAPTER 12.

IT was rather moist in the Fog Bank.

"Seems like a reg'lar drizzle," said Trot. "I'll be soaked through in a minute." She had been given a costume of blue silk, in exchange for her own dress, and the silk was so thin that the moisture easily wetted it.

"Never mind," said Cap'n Bill. "When it's a case of life 'n' death, clo's don't count for much. I'm sort o' drippy myself."

Cried the parrot, fluttering his feathers to try to keep them from sticking together:

> "Floods and gushes fill our path —
>   This is not my day for a bath!
>   Shut it off, or fear my wrath."

"We can't," laughed Trot. "We'll jus' have to stick it out till **we** get to the other side."

"Had we better go to the other side?" asked Button-Bright, anxiously.

"Why not?" returned Cap'n Bill. "The other side's the only safe side for us."

"We don't know that, sir," said the boy. "Ghip-Ghisizzle said it was a terrible country."

"I don't believe it," retorted the sailor, stoutly. "Sizzle's never been there, an' he knows nothing about it. 'The Sunset Country' sounds sort o' good to me."

"But how'll we ever manage to get there?" inquired Trot. "Aren't we already lost in this fog?"

"Not yet," said Cap'n Bill. "I've kep' my face turned straight ahead, ever since we climbed inter this bank o' wetness. If we don't get twisted any, we'll go straight through to the other side."

It was no darker in the Fog Bank than it had been in the Blue Country. They could see dimly the mass of fog, which seemed to cling to them, and when they looked down they discovered that they were walking upon white pebbles that were slightly tinged with the blue color of the sky. Gradually this blue became fainter, until, as they progressed, everything became a dull gray.

"I wonder how far it is to the other side," remarked Trot, wearily.

"We can't say till we get there, mate," answered the

sailor in a cheerful voice. Cap'n Bill had a way of growing more and more cheerful when danger threatened.

"Never mind," said the girl; "I'm as wet as a dish rag now, and I'll never get any wetter."

"Wet, wet, wet!
It's awful wet, you bet!"

moaned the parrot on her shoulder.

"I'm a fish-pond, I'm a well;
I'm a clam without a shell!"

"Can't you dry up?" asked Cap'n Bill.

"Not this evening, thank you, sir;
To talk and grumble I prefer,"

replied the parrot, dolefully.

They walked along more slowly now, still keeping hold of hands; for although they were anxious to get through the Fog Bank they were tired with the long run across the country and with their day's adventures. They had had no sleep and it was a long time past midnight.

"Look out!" cried the parrot, sharply; and they all halted to find a monstrous frog obstructing their path. Cap'n Bill thought it was as big as a whale, and as it squatted on the gray pebbles its eyes were on a level with those of the old sailor.

"Ker-chug, ker-choo!" grunted the frog; "what in the Sky is *this* crowd?"

"W — we're — strangers," stammered Trot; "an' we're tryin' to 'scape from the Blueskins an' get into the Pink Country."

"I don't blame you," said the frog, in a friendly tone. "I hate those Blueskins. The Pinkies, however, are very decent neighbors."

"Oh, I'm glad to hear that!" cried Button-Bright. "Can you tell us, Mister — Mistress — good Mr. Frog — eh — eh — your Royal Highness — if we're on the right road to the Pink Country?"

The frog seemed to laugh, for he gurgled in his throat in a very funny way.

"I'm no Royal Highness," he said. "I'm just a common frog, and a little wee tiny frog, too. But I hope to grow, in time. This Fog Bank is the Paradise of Frogs and our King is about ten times as big as I am."

"Then he's a big un, an' no mistake," admitted Cap'n Bill. "I'm glad you like your country, but it's a mite too damp for us, an' we'd be glad to get out of it."

"Follow me," said the frog. "I'll lead you to the border. It's only about six jumps."

He turned around, made a mighty leap and disappeared in the gray mist.

Our friends looked at one another in bewilderment.

"Don't see how we can foller that lead," remarked Cap'n Bill; "but we may as well start in the same direction."

"Brooks and creeks,
How it leaks!"

muttered the parrot;

"How can we jog
To a frog in a fog?"

The big frog seemed to understand their difficulty, for he kept making noises in his throat to guide them to where he had leaped. When at last they came up to him he made a second jump—out of sight, as before—and when they attempted to follow they found a huge lizard lying across the path. Cap'n Bill thought it must be a giant alligator, at first, it was so big; but he looked at them sleepily and did not seem at all dangerous.

"O, Liz—you puffy Liz—
Get out of our way and mind your biz,"

cried the parrot.

"Creep-a-mousie, crawl-a-mousie, please move on!
We can't move a step till you are gone."

"Don't disturb me," said the lizard; "I'm dreaming about parsnips. Did you ever taste a parsnip?"

"We're in a hurry, if it's the same to you, sir," said Cap'n Bill, politely.

"Then climb over me—or go around—I don't care which," murmured the lizard. "When they're little, they're juicy; when they're big, there's more of 'em; but either way there's nothing so delicious as a parsnip. There are none here in the Fog Bank, so the best I can do is dream of them. Oh, parsnips—par-snips—p-a-r-snips!" He closed his eyes sleepily and resumed his dreams.

Walking around the lizard they resumed their journey and soon came to the frog, being guided by its grunts and croaks. Then off it went again, its tremendous leap carrying it far into the fog. Suddenly Cap'n Bill tripped and would have fallen flat had not Trot and Button-Bright held him up. Then he saw that he had stumbled over the claw of a gigantic land-crab, which lay sprawled out upon the pebbly bottom.

Oh; beg parding, I'm sure!" exclaimed Cap'n Bill backing away.

"Don't mention it," replied the crab, in a tired tone. "You did not disturb me, so there is no harm done."

"We didn't know you were here," explained Trot.

"Probably not," said the crab. "It's no place for me, anyhow, for I belong in the Constellations, you know, with Taurus and Gemini and the other fellows. But I had the misfortune to tumble out of the Zodiac some time ago. My name is Cancer—but I'm not a disease. Those who examine the heavens in these days, alas! can find no Cancer there."

"Yes, we can, sir,
Mister Cancer!"

said the parrot, with a chuckle.

"Once," remarked Cap'n Bill, "I sawr a picter of you in an almanac."

"Ah; the almanacs always did us full justice," the crab replied, "but I'm told they're not fashionable now."

"If you don't mind, we'd like to pass on," said Button-Bright.

"No; I don't mind; but be careful not to step on my legs. They're rheumatic, it's so moist here."

They climbed over some of the huge legs and walked around others. Soon they had left the creature far behind.

"Aren't you rather slow?" asked the frog, when once more they came up to him.

"It isn't that," said Trot. "You are rather swift, I guess."

The frog chuckled and leaped again. They noticed that the fog had caught a soft rose tint, and was lighter and less dense than before, for which reason the sailor remarked that they must be getting near to the Pink Country.

On this jump they saw nothing but a monstrous turtle, which lay asleep with its head and legs drawn into its shell. It was not in their way, so they hurried on and rejoined the frog, which said to them:

"I'm sorry, but I'm due at the King's Court in a few minutes and I can't wait for your short, weak legs to make the journey to the Pink Country. But if you will climb upon my back I think I can carry you to the border in one more leap."

"I'm tired," said Trot, "an' this awful fog's beginnin' to choke me. Let's ride on the frog, Cap'n."

"Right you are, mate," he replied, and although he shook a bit with fear, the old man at once began to climb to the frog's back. Trot seated herself on one side of him and Button-Bright on the other, and the sailor put his arms around them both to hold them tight together.

"Are you ready?" asked the frog.

"Ding-dong!" cried the parrot;

"All aboard! let 'er go!
Jump the best jump that you know."

"Don't—don't! Jump sort o' easy, please," begged Cap'n Bill.

But the frog was unable to obey his request. Its powerful hind legs straightened like steel springs and shot the big body, with its passengers, through the fog like an arrow launched from a bow. They gasped for breath and tried to hang on, and then suddenly the frog landed just at the edge of the Fog Bank, stopping so abruptly that his three riders left his back and shot far ahead of him.

Chapter Twelve

They felt the fog melt away and found themselves bathed in glorious rays of sunshine; but they had no time to consider this change because they were still shooting through the air, and presently—before they could think of anything at all —all three were rolling heels over head on the soft grass of a meadow.

THE PINK COUNTRY

CHAPTER 13.

WHEN the travelers could collect their senses and sit up they stared about them in bewilderment, for the transition from the sticky, damp fog to this brilliant scene was so abrupt as to daze them at first.

It was a Pink Country, indeed. The grass was a soft pink, the trees were pink, all the fences and buildings which they saw in the near distance were pink—even the gravel in the pretty paths was pink. Many shades of color were there, of course, grading from a faint blush rose to deep pink verging on red, but no other color was visible. In the sky hung a pink glow, with rosy clouds floating here and there, and the sun was not silvery white, as we see it from the Earth, but a distinct pink.

The sun was high in the sky, just now, which proved the adventurers had been a long time in passing through the Fog Bank. But all of them were wonderfully relieved to reach

Chapter Thirteen

this beautiful country in safety, for aside from the danger that threatened them in the Blue Country, the other side of the island was very depressing. Here the scene that confronted them was pretty and homelike, except for the prevailing color and the fact that all the buildings were round, without a single corner or angle.

Half a mile distant was a large City, its pink tintings glistening bravely in the pink sunshine, while hundreds of pink banners floated from its numerous domes. The country between the Fog Bank and the City was like a vast garden, very carefully kept and as neat as wax.

The parrot was fluttering its wings and pruning its feathers to remove the wet of the fog. Trot and Button-Bright and Cap'n Bill were all soaked to the skin and chilled through, but as they sat upon the pink grass they felt the rays of the sun sending them warmth and rapidly drying their clothes; so, being tired out, they laid themselves comfortably down and first one and then another fell cosily asleep.

It was the parrot that aroused them.

> "Look out — look out —
> There's folks about!"

it screamed;

> "The apple-dumplings, fat and pink,
> Will be here quicker than a wink!"

131

Sky Island

Trot started up in alarm and rubbed her eyes; Cap'n Bill rolled over and blinked, hardly remembering where he was; Button-Bright was on his feet in an instant. Advancing toward them were four of the natives of the Pink Country.

Two were men and two were women, and their appearance was in sharp contrast to that of the Blueskins. For the Pinkies were round and chubby—almost like "apple-dumplings," as the parrot had called them—and they were not very tall, the highest of the men being no taller than Trot or Button-Bright. They all had short necks and legs, pink hair and eyes, rosy cheeks and pink complexions, and their faces were good-natured and jolly in expression.

The men wore picturesque pink clothing and round hats with pink feathers in them, but the apparel of the women was still more gorgeous and striking. Their dresses consisted of layer after layer of gauzy tucks and ruffles and laces, caught here and there with bows of dainty ribbon. The skirts— which of course were of many shades of pink—were so fluffy and light that they stuck out from the fat bodies of the Pinkie women like the skirts of ballet-dancers, displaying their chubby pink ankles and pink kid shoes. They wore rings and necklaces and bracelets and brooches of rose-gold set with pink gems, and all four of the new arrivals, both men and women, carried sharp-pointed sticks, made of rosewood, for weapons.

Chapter Thirteen

They halted a little way from our adventurers and one of the women muttered in a horrified voice: "Blueskins!"

"Guess again! The more you guess
I rather think you'll know the less,"

retorted the parrot; and then he added grumblingly in Trot's ear: "Blue feathers don't make bluebirds."

"Really," said the little girl, standing up and bowing respectfully to the Pinkies, "we are not Blueskins, although we are wearing the blue uniforms of the Boolooroo and have just escaped from the Blue Country. If you will look closely you will see that our skins are white."

"There is some truth in what she says," remarked one of the men, thoughtfully. "Their skins are not blue, but neither are they white. To be exact, I should call the skin of the girl and that of the boy a muddy pink, rather faded, while the skin of the gigantic monster with them is an unpleasant brown."

Cap'n Bill looked cross for a minute, for he did not like to be called a "gigantic monster," although he realized he was much larger than the pink people.

"What country did you come from?" asked the woman who had first spoken.

"From the Earth," replied Button-Bright.

"The Earth! The Earth!" they repeated. "That is a country we have never heard of. Where is it located?"

"Why, down below, somewhere," said the boy, who did

not know in which direction the Earth lay. "It isn't just one country, but a good many countries."

"We have three countries in Sky Island," returned the woman. "They are the Blue Country, the Fog Country and the Pink Country; but of course this end of the Island is the most important."

"How came you in the Blue Country, from whence you say you escaped?" asked the man.

"We flew there by means of a Magic Umbrella," explained Button-Bright; "but the wicked Boolooroo stole it from us."

"Stole it! How dreadful," they all cried in a chorus.

"And they made us slaves," said Trot.

"An' wanted fer to patch us," added Cap'n Bill, indignantly.

"So we ran away and passed through the Fog Bank and came here," said Button-Bright.

The Pinkies turned away and conversed together in low tones. Then one of the women came forward and addressed the strangers.

"Your story is the strangest we have ever heard," said she; "and your presence here is still more strange and astonishing. So we have decided to take you to Tourmaline and let her decide what shall be your fate."

"Who is Tourmaline?" inquired Trot, doubtfully, for she didn't like the idea of being "taken" to anyone.

Chapter Thirteen

"The Queen of the Pinkies. She is the sole Ruler of our country, so the word of Tourmaline is the Law of the Land."

"Seems to me we've had 'bout enough of kings an' queens," remarked Cap'n Bill. "Can't we shy your Tut—Tor—mar-line—or whatever you call her—in some way, an' deal with you direct?"

"No. Until we prove your truth and honoi we must regard you as enemies of our race. If you had a Magic Umbrella you may be magicians and sorcerers, come here to deceive us and perhaps betray us to our natural enemies, the Blueskins."

"Mud and bricks—fiddlesticks!
We don't play such nasty tricks,"

yelled the parrot, angrily, and this caused the Pinkies to shrink back in alarm, for they had never seen a parrot before.

"Surely this is magic!" declared one of the men. "No bird can talk unless inspired by witchcraft."

"Oh, yes; parrots can," said Trot.

But this incident had determined the Pinkies to consider our friends prisoners and to take them immediately before their Queen.

"Must we fight you?" asked the woman, "or will you come with us peaceably?"

"We'll go peaceable," answered Cap'n Bill. "You're a-makin' a sad mistake, for we're as harmless as doves; but seein' as you're suspicious we'd better have it out with your Queen first as last."

Their clothing was quite dry by this time, although much wrinkled and discolored by the penetrating fog, so at once they prepared to follow the Pinkies. The two men walked on either side of them, holding the pointed sticks ready to jab them if they attempted to escape, and the two women followed in the rear, also armed with sharp sticks.

So the procession moved along the pretty roadways to the City, which they soon reached. There was a strong high wall of pink marble around it and they passed through a gate made of pink metal bars and found themselves in a most delightful and picturesque town. The houses were big and substantial, all round in shape, with domed roofs and circular windows and doorways. In all the place there was but one street — a circular one that started at the gate and wound like a corkscrew toward the center of the City. It was paved with pink marble and between the street and the houses that lined both sides of it were gardens filled with pink flowers and pink grass lawns, which were shaded by pink trees and shrubbery.

As the Queen lived in the very center of the city the captives were obliged to parade the entire length of this street, and that gave all the Pink Citizens a chance to have a good look at the strangers. The Pinkies were every one short and fat and gorgeously dressed in pink attire, and their faces indicated that they were contented and happy. They were much surprised at Cap'n Bill's great size and wooden leg—two very unusual things in their experience—and the old sailor frightened more than one Pinky boy and girl and sent them scampering into the houses, where they viewed the passing procession from behind the window shutters, in comparative safety. As for the grown people, many of them got out their sharp-pointed sticks to use as weapons in case the strangers attacked them or broke away from their guards. A few, more bold than the others, followed on at the tail of the procession, and so presently they all reached an open, circular place in the exact center of the Pink City.

TOURMALINE THE POVERTY QUEEN

CHAPTER 14

THE open space which they entered was paved with pink marble and around it were two rows of large pink statues, at least life-size and beautifully sculptured. All were set upon nicely carved pink pedestals. They were, of course, statues of Pinky men and women and all had bands of pink metal around their foreheads, in the center of each band being a glistening pink jewel.

About the middle of the open space inside the statues, which appeared to be the public meeting place of the Pinkies, was a small, low house, domed like all the other houses but built of a coarse pink stone instead of the fine marble to be seen everywhere else. It had no ornamentation, being exceedingly plain in appearance. No banners floated from it; no flowers grew near it.

Chapter Fourteen

"Here," said one of their guides, as the procession halted before the little stone building, "is the palace of Tourmaline, who is our Queen."

"What! that little cabin?" exclaimed Trot.

"Of course. Did you suppose a palace would be like one of our handsome residences?" asked the woman, evidently surprised.

"I thought it would be better," said the girl. "All the palaces I've seen were splendid."

"A splendid palace!" exclaimed one of the Pinkies, and then they looked at one another in amazement and seemed to doubt that their ears had heard aright.

"These intruders are very peculiar people," remarked a man in the crowd.

"They seem very ignorant, poor things!" said another, in reply.

"Come!" commanded the woman who led the party; "you three must follow me to the presence of Tourmaline. The people must wait outside, for there is no room for them in the palace."

So they followed her through the low archway, and in a room beyond, very simply furnished, sat a young girl engaged in darning a pair of pink stockings. She was a beautiful girl of about seventeen years of age, not fat like all the rest of the Pinkies, but slender and well formed according to our own ideas of beauty. Her complexion was not a decided pink but a soft rosy tint not much deeper than that of Trot's skin. Instead of a silken gown, furbelowed like all the others they had seen women wear in this land, Tourmaline was dressed in a severely plain robe of coarse pink cloth much resembling bedticking. Across her brow, however, was a band of rose gold, in the center of which was set a luminous pink jewel which gleamed more brilliantly than a diamond. It was her badge of office, and seemed very incongruous when compared with her poor raiment and simple surroundings.

As they entered, the girl sighed and laid down her work. Her expression was patient and resigned as she faced her audience.

"What is it, Coralie?" she asked the woman.

"Here are three strange people, Tourmaline," was the reply, "who say they have entered our country through the Fog Bank. They tell a queer story of an escape from the Blue-skins, so I decided to bring them to you, that you may determine their fate."

The Queen gazed upon our friends with evident interest. She smiled—a little sadly—at Trot, seemed to approve Button-Bright's open, frank face and was quite surprised because Cap'n Bill was so much bigger than her own people.

"Are you a giant?" she asked the sailor, in a soft, sweet voice.

"No, your Majesty," he replied; "I'm only——"

Chapter Fourteen

"Majesty!" she exclaimed, flushing a deeper pink. "Are you addressing that word to me?"

"O' course, ma'am," answered Cap'n Bill; "I'm told that's the proper way to speak to a Queen."

"Perhaps you are trying to ridicule me," she continued, regarding the sailor's face closely. "There is nothing majestic about me, as you know very well. Coralie, do you consider 'majesty' a proper word to use when addressing a Queen?" she added, appealing to the Pinky woman.

"By no means," was the prompt reply.

"What shall I call her, then?" inquired Cap'n Bill.

"Just Tourmaline. That is her name, and it is sufficient," said the woman.

"The Ruler of a country ought to be treated with great respec'," declared Trot, a little indignantly, for she thought the pretty little queen was not being properly deferred to.

"Why?" asked Tourmaline, curiously.

"Because the Ruler is the mos' 'risticratic person in any land," explained the little girl. "Even in America ever'body bows low to our President, an' the Blueskins are so 'fraid o' their Boolooroo that they tremble whenever they go near him."

"But surely that is all wrong," said Tourmaline gravely. "The Ruler is appointed to protect and serve the people, and here in the Pink Country I have the full power to carry out the laws. I even decree death, when such a punishment is merited. Therefore I am a mere agent to direct the laws, which are the Will of the People, and am only a public servant, obliged constantly to guard the welfare of my subjects."

"In that case," said Button-Bright, "you're entitled to the best there is, to pay for your trouble. A powerful ruler ought to be rich and to live in a splendid palace. Your folks ought to treat you with great respect, as Trot says."

"Oh, no," responded Tourmaline quickly; "that would indeed be very wrong. Too much should never be given to anyone. If, with my great power, conferred upon me by the people, I also possessed great wealth, I might be tempted to be cruel and overbearing. In that case my subjects would justly grow envious of my superior station. If I lived as luxuriously as my people do, and had servants and costly gowns, the good Pinkies would say that their Queen had more than they themselves — and it would be true. No; our way is best. The Ruler, be it king or queen, has absolute power to rule, but no riches — no high station — no false adulation. The people have the wealth and honor, for it is their due. The Queen has nothing but the power to execute the laws, to adjust grievances and to compel order."

"What pays you, then, for all your bother?" asked Trot.

"I have one great privilege. After my death a pink marble statue of me will be set up in the Grand Court, with the statues of the other Kings and Queens who have ruled this land, and all the Pinkies in ages to come will then honor me as having been a just and upright queen. That is my reward."

"I'm sorry for you, ma'am," said Cap'n Bill. "Your pay for bein' a queen is sort o' like a life-insurance. It don't come due till after you're dead, an' then you can't get much fun out o' it."

"I did not choose to be the Queen," answered Tourmaline, simply. "A misfortune of birth placed me here and I cannot escape my fate. It is much more desirable to be a private citizen, happy and care free. But we have talked long enough of myself. Tell me who you are, and why you have come here."

Between them they told the story of how the Magic Umbrella had taken them to Sky Island, which they did not know, when they started, was anywhere in existence. Button-Bright told this, and then Trot related their adventures among the Blueskins and how the Boolooroo had stolen the umbrella and prevented them from going home again. The parrot on her shoulder kept interrupting her continually, for the mention of the Boolooroo seemed to make the bird frantic with rage.

"Naughty, naugh-ty Boo-loo-roo!
He's the worst I ev-er knew!"

the parrot repeated over and over again.

Cap'n Bill finished the story by telling of their escape

143

through the Fog Bank. "We didn't know what your Pink Country was like, o' course," he said, "but we knew it couldn't be worse than the Blue Country, an' we didn't take any stock in their stories that the Fog Bank would be the death o' us."

"Pretty wet! Pretty wet
Was the journey, you can bet!"

declared the parrot, in conclusion.

"Yes, it was wet an' sticky, all right," agreed the sailor; "but the big frog helped us an' we got through all right."

"But what can you do here?" asked Tourmaline. "You are not like my people, the Pinkies, and there is no place for you in our country."

"That's true enough," said Cap'n Bill; "but we had to go somewhere, an' this was the likeliest place we could think of. Your Sky Island ain't very big, so when we couldn't stay in the Blue Country, where ever'body hated us, or in the Fog Bank, which ain't healthy an' is too wet for humans to live in for long, we nat'rally were forced to enter the Pink Country, where we expected to find nice people."

"We *are* nice," said Tourmaline; "but it is our country —not yours—and we have no place here for strangers. In all our history you are the first people from outside our borders who have ever stepped a foot in our land. We do not hate you, as you say the Blueskins do, nor are we savage or cruel; but we do not want you here and I am really puzzled what to do with you."

"Isn't there a law to cover this case?" asked Coralie.

"I do not remember any such law," replied the queen; "but I will search in the Great Book and see if I can find anything that refers to strange people entering our land."

"If not," said the woman, "you must make a law. It is your duty."

"I know," answered Tourmaline; "but I hope such a responsibility will not fall upon my shoulders. These poor strangers are in a very uncomfortable position and I wish I could help them to get back to their own country."

"Thank you,' said Trot. "We wish so, too. Haven't you any fairies here?"

"Oh, there are fairies, of course, as there are everywhere," answered Tourmaline; "but none that we can call to our assistance, or command to do our bidding."

"How about witches?" asked Button-Bright.

"I know of one witch," said Tourmaline, thoughtfully, "but she is not very obliging. She says it makes her head ache to perform witchcraft and so she seldom indulges in it. But, if there is no other way, I may be obliged to call upon Rosalie for help. I'll look in the Great Book first. Meantime you will go home with Coralie, who will feed you and give you entertainment. To-morrow morning come to me again and then I will decree your fate."

The little Queen then picked up her stocking and began to darn the holes in it, and Coralie, without any formal parting, led the strangers from the miserable palace.

THE SUNRISE TRIBE AND THE SUNSET TRIBE

CHAPTER 15.

ALTHOUGH Trot and her comrades were still prisoners they were far more comfortable than they had been in the Blue Country. Coralie took them to her own home, where she lived in great luxury, being one of the prominent women of the Pinkies. In this country the women seemed fully as important as the men, and instead of being coddled and petted they performed their share of the work, both in public and private affairs, and were expected to fight in the wars exactly as the men did.

Our friends learned considerable about the Pinkies during that afternoon and evening, for their hostess proved kind and agreeable and frankly answered all their questions. Although this half of Sky Island was no larger than the Blue Country, being no more than two miles square, it had several hundred inhabitants. These were divided into two tribes, which were called the Sunrise Tribe and the Sunset Tribe.

147

Sky Island

The Sunrise Tribe lived in the eastern half of the Pink Country and the Sunset Tribe in the west half, and there was great rivalry between them and, sometimes, wars.

It was all a question of social importance. The Sunrise Tribe claimed that every day the sun greeted them first of all, which proved they were the most important; but, on the other hand, the Sunset Tribe claimed that the sun always deserted the other tribe and came to them, which was evidence that they were the most attractive people. On Sky Island — at least on the Pink side — the sun arose in wonderful splendor, but also it set in a blaze of glory, and so there were arguments on both sides and for want of something better to argue about, the Pinkies took this queer subject as a cause of dispute.

Both Tribes acknowledged Tourmaline their Queen and obeyed the laws of the country, and just at this time there was peace in the land and all the inhabitants of the east and west were friendly. But they had been known, Coralie said, to fight one another fiercely with the sharp sticks, at which times a good many were sure to get hurt.

"Why do they call this an Island?" asked Button-Bright. "There isn't any water around it, is there?"

"No, but there is sky all around it," answered Coralie; "and, if one should step off the edge, he would go tumbling into the great sky and never be heard of again."

"Is there a fence around the edge?" asked Trot.

"Only a few places are fenced," was the reply. "Usually

there are rows of thick bushes set close to the edge, to prevent people from falling off. Once there was a King of the Pinkies who was cruel and overbearing and imagined he was superior to the people he ruled, so one day his subjects carried him to the edge of the island and threw him over the bushes."

"Goodness me!" said Trot. "He might have hit some one on the Earth."

"Guess he skipped it, though," added Cap'n Bill, "for I never heard of a Pinky till I came here."

"And I have never heard of the Earth," retorted Coralie. "Of course there must be such a place, because you came from there, but the Earth is never visible in our sky."

"No," said Button-Bright, "'cause it's *under* your island. But it's there, all right, and it's a pretty good place to live. I wish I could get back to it."

"So do I, Button-Bright!" exclaimed Trot.

"Let's fly!" cried the parrot, turning his head so that one bright little eye looked directly into the girl's eye. "Say good-bye and let's fly through the sky, far and high!"

"If we only had my umbrella, we'd fly in a minute," sighed Button-Bright. "But the Boolooroo stole it."

"Naugh-ty, naugh-ty Boo-loo-roo;
What a wicked thing to do!"

wailed the parrot; and they all agreed with him.

149

Coralie belonged to the Sunset Tribe, as she lived west of the queen's palace, which was the center of the Pink Country. A servant came to the room where they were conversing, to state that the sun was about to set, and at once Coralie arose and took the strangers to an upper balcony, where all the household had assembled.

The neighboring houses also had their balconies and roofs filled with people, for it seemed all the Sunset Tribe came out every night to witness the setting of the sun. It was really a magnificent sight and Trot scarcely breathed as the great golden ball sank low in the sky and colored all the clouds with gorgeous tints of orange, red and yellow. Never on the Earth was there visible such splendor, and as the little girl watched the ever-changing scene she decided the Sunset Tribe was amply justified in claiming that the West was the favored country of the sun.

"You see," said Cap'n Bill, "the sky is all around us, an' we're high up; so the sun really loses itself in the clouds an' leaves a trail of beauty behind him."

"He does that!" agreed Trot. "This is almost worth comin' for, Cap'n."

"But not quite," said Button-Bright, sadly. "I'd get along without the sunset if only we could go home."

They went in to dinner, after this, and sat at Coralie's own table, with her husband and children, and found the meal very good. After a pleasant evening, during which no reference was made to their being prisoners, they were shown to prettily furnished rooms — all in pink — and slept soundly in the soft beds provided for them.

Trot wakened early the next morning and went out on the balcony to see the sunrise. The little girl was well repaid, for the splendor of the rising sun was almost equal to that of the setting sun. Surely this was a wonderful country and much more delightful than the Blue side of the island, where the sun was hidden by the great Fog Bank and only the moon was visible.

When she went in she found that both Button-Bright and Cap'n Bill were up and dressed, so they decided to take a walk before breakfast. No one restrained them or interfered with them in any way.

"They know we can't get away," observed the sailor, "so they don't need to watch us."

"We could go into the Fog Bank again," suggested Trot.

"We could, mate, but we won't," answered Cap'n Bill. "If there's no way for us to get clean off'n Sky Island, I'd rather stay with the Pinkies than with the Blues."

"I wonder what they'll do with us," said Button-Bright. "The Queen seems like a nice girl and I don't think she'll hurt us, whatever happens."

They walked freely along the circular street, seeing such sights as the Pink City afforded, and then returned to Coralie's house for breakfast. Coralie herself was not there, as

153

she had been summoned to the Queen's palace, but her husband looked after the guests and when breakfast was finished he said to them:

"I am to take you to Tourmaline, who has promised to decide your fate this morning. I am curious to know what she will do with you, for in all our history we have never before had strangers intrude upon us."

"We're curious, too," said Trot; "but we'll soon find out."

As they walked down the street they observed that the sky was now covered with dark clouds, which entirely hid the sun.

"Does it ever rain here?" inquired Button-Bright.

"Certainly," answered Coralie's husband; "that is the one drawback of our country; it rains quite often, and although it makes the flowers and the grass grow I think rain is very disagreeable. I am always glad to see the rainbow, which is a sign that the sun will shine again."

"Looks like rain now," remarked Cap'n Bill.

"It does," said the man, glancing at the sky. "We must hurry, or we may get wet."

"Haven't you any umbrellas?" asked Button-Bright.

"No; we don't know what umbrellas are," replied the Pinky man.

It did not rain at once and they reached Tourmaline's wretched hut in safety. There they found quite a number of

Pinkies assembled, and a spirited discussion was taking place when they arrived.

"Come in, please," said Tourmaline, opening the door for them, and when they had entered she placed a pinkwood bench for them to sit upon and went back to her throne, which was a common rocking-chair.

At her right were seated six men and women of the Sunrise Tribe and on her left six men and women of the Sunset Tribe, among the latter being Coralie. The contrast between the plain, simple dress of the Queen and the gorgeous apparel of her Counselors was quite remarkable, yet her beauty far surpassed that of any of her people and her demeanor was so modest and unassuming that it was difficult for the prisoners to believe that her word could decree life or death and that all the others were subservient to her. Tourmaline's eyes were so deep a shade of pink that they were almost hazel, and her hair was darker than that of the others, being a golden-red in color. These points, taken with her light pink skin and slender form, rendered her distinctive among the Pinkies, whatever gown she might wear.

When the strangers were seated she turned to them and said:

"I have searched through the Great Book of Laws and found nothing about foreign people entering our land. There is a law that if any of the Blueskins break through the Fog Bank they shall be driven back with sharp sticks; but you are not Blueskins, so this Law does not apply to you. Therefore, in order to decide your fate, I have summoned a Council of twelve of my people, who will vote as to whether you shall be permitted to remain here or not. They wanted to see you before they cast their final vote, that they may examine you carefully and discover if you are worthy to become inhabitants of the Pink Country."

"The rose is red, the violet's blue,
But Trot is sweeter than the two!"

declared the parrot in a loud voice. It was a little verse Cap'n Bill had taught the bird that very morning, while Trot was seeing the sun rise.

The Pinkies were startled and seemed a little frightened at hearing a bird speak so clearly. Trot laughed and patted the bird's head in return for the compliment.

"Is the Monster Man whose legs are part wood a dangerous creature?" asked one of the Sunrise Tribe.

"Not to my friends," replied Cap'n Bill, much amused. "I s'pose I could fight your whole crowd o' Pinkies, if I had to, an' make you run for your lives; but bein' as you're friendly to us you ain't in any danger."

The sailor thought this speech was diplomatic and might "head off any trouble," but the Pinkies seemed uneasy and several of them picked up their slender, pointed sticks and held them in their hands. They were not cowardly, but it was evident they mistrusted the big man, who on Earth was not considered big at all, but rather undersized.

"What we'd like," said Trot, "is to stay here, cosy an' peaceable, till we can find a way to get home to the Earth again. Your country is much nicer than the Blue Country, and we like you pretty well, from what we've seen of you; so, if you'll let us stay, we won't be any more trouble to you than we can help."

They all gazed upon the little girl curiously, and one of them said:

"How strangely light her color is! And it is pink, too, which is in her favor. But her eyes are of that dreadful blue tint which prevails in the other half of Sky Island, while her hair is a queer color all unknown to us. She is not like our people and would not harmonize with the universal color here."

"That's true," said another; "the three strangers are all inharmonious. If allowed to remain here they would ruin the color scheme of the country, where all is now pink."

"In spite of that," said Coralie, "they are harmless creatures and have done us no wrong."

"Yes, they have," replied a nervous little Sunrise man; "they wronged us by coming here."

"They could not help doing that," argued Coralie, "and it is their misfortune that they are here on Sky Island at all.

Perhaps, if we keep them with us for awhile, they may find a way to return safely to their own country."

"We'll fly through the sky by-and-by—ki-yi!" yelled the parrot with startling suddenness.

"It that true?" asked a Pinky, seriously.

"Why, we would if we could," answered Trot. "We flew to this island, anyhow."

"Perhaps," said another, "if we pushed them off the edge they could fly down again. Who knows?"

"We know," answered Cap'n Bill hastily. "We'd tumble, but we wouldn't fly."

> "They'd take a fall—
> And that is all!"

observed the parrot, fluttering its wings.

There was silence for a moment, while all the Pinkies seemed to think deeply. Then the Queen asked the strangers to step outside while they counseled together. Our friends obeyed, and leaving the room they entered the courtyard and examined the rows of pink marble statues for nearly an hour before they were summoned to return to the little room in Tourmaline's palace.

"We are now ready to vote as to your fate," said the pretty Queen to them. "We have decided there are but two things for us to do: either permit you to remain here as honored guests or take you to an edge of the island and throw you over the bushes into the sky."

They were silent at hearing this dreadful alternative, but the parrot screamed shrilly:

"Oh, what a dump! Oh, what a jump!
Won't we all thump when we land with a bump?"

"If we do," said Cap'n Bill, thoughtfully, "we'll none of us know it."

ROSALIE THE WITCH

CHAPTER 16.

TROT and Button-Bright had now become worried and anxious, for they knew if they were tossed over the edge of the island they would be killed. Cap'n Bill frowned and set his jaws tight together. The old sailor had made up his mind to make a good fight for his boy and girl, as well as for his own life, if he was obliged to do so.

The twelve Counselors then voted, and when the vote was counted Tourmaline announced that six had voted to allow the strangers to remain and six to toss them over the bushes.

"We seem evenly divided on this matter," remarked the Queen, with a puzzled look at her Council.

Trot thought the pretty Queen was their friend, so she said:

"Of course you'll have the deciding vote, then, you being the Ruler."

"Oh, no," replied Tourmaline. "Since I have asked these good people to advise me it would be impolite to side against some of them and with the others. That would imply that the judgment of some of my Counselors is wrong, and the judgment of others right. I must ask some one else to cast the deciding vote."

"Who will it be, then?" inquired Trot. "Can't I do it? Or Cap'n Bill, or Button-Bright?"

Tourmaline smiled and shook her head, while all the Counselors murmured their protests.

"Let Trot do it
Or you'll rue it!"

advised the parrot, and then he barked like a dog and made them all jump.

"Let me think a moment," said the Queen, resting her chin on her hand.

"A Pink can think
As quick's a wink!"

the parrot declared.

But Tourmaline's thoughts required time and all her Counselors remained silent and watched her anxiously.

At last she raised her head and said:

"I shall call upon Rosalie the Witch. She is wise and honest and will decide the matter justly."

Sky Island

The Pinkies seemed to approve this choice, so Tourmaline rose and took a small pink paper parcel from a drawer. In it was a pink powder which she scattered upon the seat of a big armchair. Then she lighted this powder, which at first flashed vivid pink and then filled all the space around the chair with a thick pink cloud of smoke. Presently the smoke cleared away, when they all saw seated within the chair Rosalie the Witch.

This famous woman was much like the other Pinkies in appearance except that she was somewhat taller and not quite so fat as most of the people. Her skin and hair and eyes were all of a rosy pink color and her gown was of spider-web gauze that nicely matched her complexion. She did not seem very old, for her features were smiling and attractive and pleasant to view. She held in her hand a slender staff tipped with a lustrous pink jewel.

All the Pinkies present bowed very respectfully to Rosalie, who returned the salutation with a dignified nod. Then Tourmaline began to explain the presence of the three strangers and the difficulty of deciding what to do with them.

"I have summoned you here that you may cast the deciding vote," added the Queen. "What shall we do, Rosalie: allow them to remain here as honored guests, or toss them over the bushes into the sky?"

Rosalie, during Tourmaline's speech, had been attentively examining the faces of the three Earth people. Now she said:

"Before I decide I must see who these strangers are. I will follow their adventures in a vision, to discover if they have told you the truth. And, in order that you may all share my knowledge, you shall see the vision as I see it."

She then bowed her head and closed her eyes.

"Rock-a-bye, baby, on a tree-top;
Don't wake her up or the vision will stop,"

muttered the parrot; but no one paid any attention to the noisy bird.

Gradually a pink mist formed in the air about the Witch and in this mist the vision began to appear.

First, there was Button-Bright in the attic of his house, finding the Magic Umbrella. Then his first flight was shown, and afterward his trip across the United States until he landed on the bluff where Trot sat. In rapid succession the scenes shifted and disclosed the trial flights, with Trot and Cap'n Bill as passengers, then the trip to Sky Island and the meeting with the Boolooroo. No sound was heard, but it was easy from the gestures of the actors for the Pinkies to follow all the adventures of the strangers in the Blue Country. Button-Bright was greatly astonished to see in this vision how the Boolooroo had tested the Magic Umbrella and in a fit of rage cast it into a corner underneath the cabinet, with the seats and lunch basket still attached to the handle by means of the rope. The boy now knew why he could not find the umbrella in the Treasure Chamber, and he was provoked to think he had several times been quite close to it without knowing it was there. The last scene ended with the trip through the Fog Bank and the assistance rendered them by the friendly frog. After the three tumbled upon the grass of the Pink Country the vision faded away and Rosalie lifted her head with a smile of triumph at the success of her witchcraft.

"Did you see clearly?" she asked.

"We did, O Wonderful Witch!" they declared.

"Then," said Rosalie, "there can be no doubt in your minds that these strangers have told you the truth."

"None at all," they admitted.

"What arguments are advanced by the six Counselors who voted to allow them to remain here as guests?" inquired the Witch.

"They have done us no harm," answered Coralie, speaking for her side; "therefore we should, in honor and justice, do them no harm."

Rosalie nodded. "What arguments have the others advanced?" she asked.

"They interfere with our color scheme, and do not harmonize with our people," a man of the Sunrise Tribe answered.

Again Rosalie nodded, and Trot thought her eyes twinkled a little.

Chapter Sixteen

"I think I now fully comprehend the matter," said she, "and so I will cast my vote. I favor taking the Earth people to the edge of the island and casting them into the sky."

For a moment there was perfect silence in the room. All present realized that this was a decree of death to the strangers.

Trot was greatly surprised at the decision and for a moment she thought her heart had stopped beating, for a wave of fear swept over her. Button-Bright flushed red as a Pinky and then grew very pale. He crept closer to Trot and took her hand in his own, pressing it to give the little girl courage. As for Cap'n Bill, he was watching the smiling face of the Witch in a puzzled but not hopeless way, for he thought she did not seem wholly in earnest in what she had said.

"The case is decided," announced Tourmaline, in a clear, cold voice. "The three strangers shall be taken at once to the edge of the island and thrown over the bushes into the sky."

"It's raining hard outside," announced Coralie, who sat near the door; "why not wait until this shower is over?"

"I have said 'at once'," replied the little Queen, with dignity, "and so it must be at once. We are accustomed to rain, so it need not delay us, and when a disagreeable duty is to be performed the sooner it is accomplished the better."

"May I ask, ma'am," said Cap'n Bill, addressing the Witch, "why you have decided to murder of us in this cold-blooded way?"

"I did not decide to murder you," answered Rosalie.

"To throw us off the island will be murder," declared the sailor.

"Then they cannot throw you off," the Witch replied.

"The Queen says they will."

"I know," said Rosalie; "but I'm quite positive her people can't do it."

This statement astonished all the Pinkies, who looked at the Witch inquiringly.

"Why not?" asked Tourmaline.

"It is evident to me," said the Witch, speaking slowly and distinctly, "that these Earth people are protected in some way by fairies. They may not be aware of this themselves, nor did I see any fairies in my vision. But, if you will think upon it carefully, you will realize that the Magic Umbrella has no power in itself, but is enchanted by fairy powers, so that it is made to fly and to carry passengers through the air *by fairies*. This being the case, I do not think you will be allowed to injure these favored people in any way; but I am curious to see in what manner the fairies will defend them, and therefore I voted to have them thrown off the island. I bear these strangers no ill will, nor do I believe they are in any danger. But since you, Tourmaline, have determined to attempt this terrible thing at once, I shall go with you and see what will happen."

Chapter Sixteen

Some of the Pinkies looked pleased and some troubled at this speech, but they all prepared to escort the prisoners to the nearest edge of the island. The rain was pouring down in torrents and umbrellas were unknown; but all of them, both men and women, slipped gossamer raincoats over their clothing which kept the rain from wetting them. Then they caught up their sharp sticks and, surrounding the doomed captives, commanded them to march to meet their fate.

THE ARRIVAL OF POLYCHROME

CHAPTER 17.

CAP'N BILL had determined to fight desperately for their lives, but he was a shrewd old sailorman and he found much that was reasonable in the Witch's assertion that fairies would protect them. He had often wondered how the Magic Umbrella could fly and obey spoken commands, but now he plainly saw that the thing must be directed by some invisible power, and that power was quite likely to save them from the cruel death that had been decreed. To be sure, the Magic Umbrella was now in the Blue Country, and the fairies that directed its flight might be with the umbrella instead of with them, yet the old sailor had already experienced some strange adventures in Trot's company and knew she had managed to escape every danger that had threatened. So he decided not to fight until the last moment, and meekly hobbled along the street, as he was commanded to do. Trot was also encouraged by the Witch's suggestion, for she believed in fairies and trusted them; but Button-Bright could find no comfort in their situation and his face was very sad as he marched along by Trot's side.

If they had followed the corkscrew windings of the street it would have been a long journey to the outer edge of the Pink Country, but Tourmaline took a short cut, leading them through private gardens and even through houses, so that they followed almost a bee line to their destination. It rained all the way and the walking was very disagreeable; but our friends were confronting an important crisis in their strange adventures and with possible death at their journey's end they were in no hurry to arrive there.

Once free of the City they traversed the open country, and here they often stepped into sticky pink mud up to their ankles. Cap'n Bill's wooden leg would often go down deep and stick fast in this mud, and at such times he would be help-less until two of the Pinkies — who were a strong people — pulled him out again.

The parrot was getting its feathers sadly draggled in the rain and the poor bird soon presented a wet and woebegone appearance.

> "Soak us again —
> Drown us with rain!"

it muttered in a resigned tone; and then it would turn to Trot and moan:

> "The rose is red, the violet's blue;
> The Pinkies are a beastly crew!"

The country was not so trim and neatly kept near the edge, for it was evident the people did not care to go too near to the dangerous place. There was a row of thick bushes, which concealed the gulf below, and as they approached these bushes the rain abruptly ceased and the clouds began to break and drift away in the sky.

"Two of you seize the girl and throw her over," said Tourmaline, in a calm, matter-of-fact way, "and two others must throw the boy over. It may take four, perhaps, to lift the huge and ancient man."

"More'n that," said Cap'n Bill, grimly. "I'm pretty sure it'll take all o' you, young lady, an' the chances are you won't do it then."

They had halted a short distance from the bushes and now there suddenly appeared through a rift in the clouds an immense Rainbow. It was perfectly formed and glistened with a dozen or more superb tintings that were so vivid and brilliant and blended into one another so exquisitely that every one paused to gaze enraptured upon the sight.

Steadily, yet with wonderful swiftness, the end of the great bow descended until it rested upon the pink field — almost at the feet of the little party of observers. Then they saw, dancing gaily upon the arch, a score of beautiful maidens, dressed in fleecy robes of rainbow tints which fluttered around them like clouds.

"The Daughters of the Rainbow!" whispered Tourmaline, in an awed voice, and the Witch beside her nodded and said: "Fairies of the sky. What did I tell you, Tourmaline?"

"Just then one of the maidens tripped lightly down the span of the arch until near the very end, leaning over to observe the group below. She was exquisitely fair, dainty as a lily and graceful as a bough swaying in the breeze.

"Why, it's Polychrome!" exclaimed Button-Bright, in a voice of mingled wonder and delight. "Hello, Polly! Don't you remember me?"

"Of course I remember Button-Bright," replied the maiden, in a sweet, tinkling voice. "The last time I saw you was in the Land of Oz."

"Oh!" cried Trot, turning to stare at the boy with big, wide-open eyes; "were you ever in the Land of Oz?"

"Yes," he answered, still looking at the Rainbow's Daughter; and then he said appealingly: "These people want to kill us, Polly. Can't you help us?"

"Polly wants a cracker!—Polly wants a cracker!" screeched the parrot.

Polychrome straightened up and glanced at her sisters.

"Tell Father to call for me in an hour or two," said she.

Sky Island

"There is work for me to do here, for one of my old friends is in trouble."

With this she sprang lightly from the rainbow and stood beside Button-Bright and Trot, and scarcely had she left the splendid arch when it lifted and rose into the sky. The other end had been hidden in the clouds and now the Rainbow began to fade gradually, like mist, and the sun broke through the clouds and shot its cheering rays over the Pink Country until presently the Rainbow had vanished altogether and the only reminder of it was the lovely Polychrome standing among the wondering band of Pinkies.

"Tell me," she said gently to the boy, "why are you here, and why do these people of the sky wish to destroy you?"

In a few hurried words Button-Bright related their adventure with the Magic Umbrella, and how the Boolooroo had stolen it and they had been obliged to escape into the Pink Country.

Polychrome listened and then turned to the Queen.

"Why have you decreed death to these innocent strangers?" she asked.

"They do not harmonize with our color scheme," replied Tourmaline.

"That is utter nonsense," declared Polychrome, impatiently. "You're so dreadfully pink here that your color, which in itself is beautiful, has become tame and insipid. What you really need is some sharp contrast to enhance the charm of your country, and to keep these three people with you would be a benefit rather than an injury to you."

At this the Pinkies looked downcast and ashamed, while only Rosalie the Witch laughed and seemed to enjoy the rebuke.

"But," protested Tourmaline, "the Great Book of Laws says our country shall harbor none but the Pinkies."

"Does it, indeed?" asked the Rainbow's Daughter. "Come, let us return at once to your City and examine your Book of Laws. I am quite sure I can find in them absolute protection for these poor wanderers."

They dared not disobey Polychrome's request, so at once they all turned and walked back to the City. As it was still muddy underfoot the Rainbow's Daughter took a cloak from one of the women, partly rolled it and threw it upon the ground. Then she stepped upon it and began walking forward. The cloak unrolled as she advanced, affording a constant carpet for her feet and for those of the others who followed her. So, being protected from the mud and wet, they speedily gained the City and in a short time were all gathered in the low room of Tourmaline's palace, where the Great Book of Laws lay upon a table.

Polychrome began turning over the leaves, while the others all watched her anxiously and in silence.

"Here," she said presently, "is a Law which reads as follows: 'Everyone in the Pink Country is entitled to the protection of the Ruler and to a house and a good living, except only the Blueskins. If any of the natives of the Blue Country should ever break through the Fog Bank they must be driven back with sharp sticks.' Have you read this Law, Tourmaline?"

"Yes," said the Queen; "but how does that apply to these strangers?"

"Why, being in the Pink Country, as they surely are, and not being Blueskins, they are by this Law entitled to protection, to a home and good living. The Law does not say 'Pinkies,' it says any who are in the Pink Country."

"True," agreed Coralie, greatly pleased, and all the other Pinkies nodded their heads and repeated: "True—true!"

"The rose is red, the violet's blue,
The law's the thing, because it's true!"

cried the parrot.

"I am indeed relieved to have you interpret the Law in this way," declared Tourmaline. "I knew it was cruel to throw these poor people over the edge, but that seemed to us the only thing to be done."

"It was cruel and unjust," answered Polychrome, as sternly as her sweet voice could speak. "But here," she added, for she had still continued to turn the leaves of the Great Book, "is another Law which you have also overlooked. It says: 'The person, whether man or woman, boy or girl, living in the Pink Country who has the lightest skin, shall be the Ruler — King or Queen — as long as he or she lives, unless some one of a lighter skin is found, and this Ruler's commands all the people must obey.' Do you know this Law?"

"Oh, yes," replied Tourmaline. "That is why I am the Queen. You will notice my complexion is of a lighter pink than that of any other of my people."

"Yes," remarked Polychrome, looking at her critically, "when you were made Queen without doubt you had the lightest colored skin in all the Pink Country. But now you are no longer Queen of the Pinkies, Tourmaline."

Those assembled were so startled by this statement that they gazed at the Rainbow's Daughter in astonishment for a time. Then Tourmaline asked:

"Why not, your Highness?"

"Because here is one lighter in color than yourself," pointing to Trot. "This girl is, by the Law of the Great Book, the rightful Queen of the Pinkies, and as loyal citizens you are all obliged to obey her commands. Give me that circlet from your brow, Tourmaline."

Without hesitation Tourmaline removed the rose-gold circlet with its glittering jewel and handed it to Polychrome, who turned and placed it upon Trot's brow. Then she called in a loud, imperative voice:

"Greet your new Queen, Pinkies!"

One by one they all advanced, knelt before Trot and pressed her hand to their lips.

"Long live Queen Mayre!" called out Cap'n Bill, dancing around on his wooden leg in great delight; "vive la — vive la — ah, ah — Trot!"

"Thank you, Polly," said Button-Bright gratefully. "This will fix us all right, I'm sure."

"Why, I have done nothing," returned Polychrome, smiling upon him; "it is the Law of the Country. Isn't it surprising how little most people know of their Laws? Are you all contented, Pinkies?" she asked, turning to the people.

"We are!" they cried. Then several of the men ran out to spread the news throughout the City and Country, so that a vast crowd soon began to gather in the Court of the Statues.

MAYRE, QUEEN OF THE PINK COUNTRY

CHAPTER 18.

POLYCHROME now dismissed all but Button-Bright, Cap'n Bill, Rosalie the Witch and the new Queen of the Pinkies. Tourmaline hastened away to her father's house to put on a beautiful gown all covered with flounces and ribbons, for she was glad to be relieved of the duties of Queen and was eager to be gaily dressed and one of the people again.

"I s'pose," said Trot, "I'll have to put on one of Tourmaline's common pink dresses."

"Yes," replied Polychrome, "you must follow the customs of the country, absurd though they may be. In the little sleeping chamber adjoining this room you will find plenty of gowns poor enough for the Queen to wear. Shall I assist you to put one on?"

"No," answered Trot, "I guess I can manage it alone."

When she withdrew to the little chamber the Rainbow's

Daughter began conversing with the Witch, whom she urged to stay with the new queen and protect her as long as she ruled the Pink Country. Rosalie, who longed to please the powerful Polychrome, whose fairy powers as Daughter of the Rainbow were far superior to her own witchcraft, promised faithfully to devote herself to Queen Mayre as long as she might need her services.

By the time Trot was dressed in pink, and had returned to the room, there was an excited and clamorous crowd assembled in the court, and Polychrome took the little girl's hand and led her out to greet her new subjects.

The Pinkies were much impressed by the fact that the Rainbow's Daughter was their new Queen's friend, and that Rosalie the Witch stood on Trot's left hand and treated her with humble deference. So they shouted their approval very enthusiastically and pressed forward one by one to kneel before their new Ruler and kiss her hand.

The parrot was now on Cap'n Bill's shoulder, for Trot thought a Queen ought not to carry a bird around; but the parrot did not mind the change and was as much excited as anyone in the crowd.

"Oh, what bliss to kiss a miss!" he shouted, as Trot held out her hand to be kissed by her subjects; and then he would scream:

> "We're in the sky and flyin' high:
> We're goin' to live instead of die,

180

It's time to laugh instead of cry;
Oh, my! ki-yi! ain't this a pie!'"

Cap'n Bill let the bird jabber as he pleased, for the occasion was a joyful one and it was no wonder the parrot was excited.

And, while the throng shouted greetings to the Queen, suddenly the great Rainbow appeared in the sky and dropped its end right on the Court of the Statues. Polychrome stooped to kiss Trot and Button-Bright, gave Cap'n Bill a charming smile and Rosalie the Witch a friendly nod of farewell. Then she sprang lightly upon the arch of the Rainbow and was greeted by the bevy of dancing, laughing maidens who were her sisters.

"I shall keep watch over you, Button-Bright," she called to the boy. "Don't despair, whatever happens, for behind the clouds is always the Rainbow!"

"Thank you, Polly," he answered, and Trot also thanked the lovely Polychrome—and so did Cap'n Bill. The parrot made quite a long speech, flying high above the arch where Polychrome stood and then back to Cap'n Bill's shoulder. Said he:

"We Pollys know our business, and we're—all—right!
We'll take good care of Cap'n Bill and Trot and Button-
    Bright

You watch 'em from the Rainbow, and I'll watch day and
 night,
And we'll call a sky policeman if trouble comes in sight!"

Suddenly the bow lifted and carried the dancing maidens
into the sky. The colors faded, the arch slowly dissolved and
the heavens were clear.

Trot turned to the Pinkies.

"Let's have a holiday to-day," she said. "Have a good
time and enjoy yourselves. I don't jus' know how I'm goin'
to rule this country, yet, but I'll think it over an' let you
know."

Then she went into the palace hut with Cap'n Bill and
Button-Bright and Rosalie the Witch, and the people went
away to enjoy themselves and talk over the surprising events
of the day.

"Dear me," said Trot, throwing herself into a chair,
"wasn't that a sudden change of fortune, though? That
Rainbow's Daughter is a pretty good fairy. I'm glad you
knew her, Button-Bright."

"I was sure something would happen to save you," remarked Rosalie, "and that was why I voted to have you
thrown off the edge. I wanted to discover who would come
to your assistance, and I found out. Now I have made a
friend of Polychrome and that will render me more powerful

as a Witch, for I can call upon her for assistance whenever I need her."

"But—see here," said Cap'n Bill; "you can't afford to spend your time a-rulin' this tucked-up country, Trot."

"Why not?" asked Trot, who was pleased with her new and important position.

"It'd get pretty tiresome, mate, after you'd had a few quarrels with the Pinkies, for they expec' their Queen to be as poor as poverty an' never have any fun in life."

"You wouldn't like it for long, I'm sure," added Button-Bright, seriously.

Trot seemed thoughtful.

"No; I don't know's I would," she admitted. "But as long as we stay here it seems a pretty good thing to be Queen. I guess I'm a little proud of it. I wish mother could see me rulin' the Pinkies—an' Papa Griffith, too. Wouldn't they open their eyes?"

"They would, mate; but they can't see you," said Cap'n Bill. "So the question is, what's to be done?"

"We ought to get home," observed the boy. "Our folks will worry about us and Earth's the best place to live, after all. If we could only get hold of my Magic Umbrella, we'd be all right."

"The rose is red, the violet's blue,
But the umbrel's stole by the Boo-loo-roo!"

screamed the parrot.

"That's it," said Cap'n Bill; "the Boolooroo's got the umbrel, an' that settles the question."

"Tell me," said Rosalie; "if you had your Magic Umbrella, could you fly home again in safety?"

"Of course we could," replied Button-Bright.

"And would you prefer to go home to remaining here?"

"We would, indeed!"

"Then why do you not get the umbrella?"

"How?" asked Trot, eagerly.

The Witch paused a moment. Then she said:

"You must go into the Blue Country and force the Boolooroo to give up your property."

"Through the Fog Bank?" asked Cap'n Bill, doubtfully.

"And let the Boolooroo capture us again?" demanded Button-Bright, with a shiver.

"An' have to wait on the Snubnoses instead of bein' a Queen!" said Trot.

"You must remember that conditions have changed, and you are now a powerful Ruler," replied Rosalie. "The Pinkies are really a great nation, and they are pledged to obey your commands. Why not assemble an army, march through the Fog Bank, fight and conquer the Boolooroo and recapture the Magic Umbrella?"

"Hooray!" shouted Cap'n Bill, pounding his wooden leg on the floor; "that's the proper talk! Let's do it, Queen Trot."

"It doesn't seem like a bad idea," added Button-Bright.

"Do you think the Pinkies could fight the Blueskins?" asked Trot.

"Why not?" replied the sailorman. "They have sharp sticks, an' know how to use 'em, whereas the Blueskins have only them windin'-up cords, with weights on the ends."

"The Blueskins are the biggest people," said the girl.

"But they're cowards, I'm sure," declared the boy.

"Anyhow," the sailor remarked, "that's our only hope of ever gett'n' home again. I'd like to try it, Trot."

"If you decide on this adventure," said Rosalie, "I believe I can be of much assistance to you."

"That'll help," asserted Cap'n Bill.

"And we've one good friend among the Blueskins," said Button-Bright. "I'm sure Ghip-Ghisizzle will side with us, and I've got the Royal Record Book, which proves that the Boolooroo has already reigned his lawful three hundred years."

"Does the book say that?" inquired Trot, with interest.

"Yes; I've been reading it."

"Then Sizzle'll be the new Boolooroo," said the girl, "an' p'raps we won't have to fight, after all."

"We'd better go prepared, though," advised Cap'n Bill, "fer that awful ol' Boolooroo won't give up without a struggle. When shall we start?"

Trot hesitated, so they all looked to Rosalie for advice.

Sky Island

"Just as soon as we can get the army together and ready," decided the Witch. "That will not take long — perhaps two or three days."

"Good!" cried Cap'n Bill, and the parrot screamed:

"Here's a lovely how-d'y'-do —
We're going to fight the Boo-loo-roo!
We'll get the Six Snubnoses, too,
And make 'em all feel mighty blue."

"Either that or the other thing," said Trot. "Anyhow, we're in for it."

THE WAR OF THE PINKS AND BLUES

CHAPTER 19.

MUCH to the surprise of the Earth people the Pinkies made no objection whatever to undertaking the adventure. Their lives were so monotonous and uninteresting that they welcomed anything in the way of excitement. This march through the unknown Fog Bank to fight the unknown Blueskins aroused them to enthusiasm, and although the result of the expedition could not be foretold and some of them were almost certain to get hurt, they did not hesitate to undertake the war.

It appeare l that Coralie was Captain of the Sunset Tribe and a man named Tintint the Captain of the Sunrise Tribe. Tintint had a very pink skin and eyes so faded in their pink color that he squinted badly in order to see anything around him. He was a fat and pompous little fellow and loved to strut up and down his line of warriors twirling his long pointed stick so that all might admire him.

Sky Island

By Rosalie's advice the Army of Conquest consisted of one hundred Sunsets and one hundred Sunrises. Many more were eager to go, but the Witch thought that would be enough. The warriors consisted of both men and women, equally divided, and there was no need to provide uniforms for them because their regular pink clothing was a distinctive uniform in itself. Each one bore a long pointed stick as the main weapon and had two short pointed sticks stuck in his belt.

While the army was getting ready, Rosalie the Witch went to the central edge of the Fog Bank and fearlessly entered it. There she called for the King of the Giant Frogs, who came at her bidding, and the two held an earnest and long talk together.

Meantime Cap'n Bill had the army assembled in the Court of the Statues, where Queen Mayre appeared and told the Pinkies that the sailorman was to be Commander in Chief of the Expedition and all must obey his commands. Then Cap'n Bill addressed the army and told what the Fog Bank was like. He advised them all to wear their rain-coats over their pretty pink clothes, so they would not get wet, and he assured them that all the creatures to be met with in the Fog were perfectly harmless.

"When we come to the Blue Country, though," he added, "you're liable to be pretty busy. The Blueskins are tall an' lanky, an' ugly an' fierce, an' if they happen to capture you,

188

you'll all be patched — which is a deep disgrace an' a uncomfertable mix-up."

"Will they throw us over the edge?" asked Captain Tintint, nervously.

"I don't think it," replied Cap'n Bill. "While I was there I never heard the edge mentioned. They're cruel enough to do that — 'specially the Boolooroo — but I guess they've never thought o' throwin' folks over the edge. They fight with long cords that have weights on the ends, which coil 'round you an' make you helpless in a jiffy; so whenever they throw them cords you mus' ward 'em off with your long sticks. Don't let 'em wind around your bodies, or you're done for."

He told them other things about the Blueskins, so they would not be frightened when they faced the enemy and found them so different in appearance from themselves, and also he assured them that the Pinkies were so much the braver and better armed that he had no doubt they would easily conquer.

On the third day, just at sunrise, the army moved forward to the Fog Bank, headed by Cap'n Bill, clad in an embroidered pink coat with wide, flowing pink trousers, and accompanied by Trot and Button-Bright and Rosalie the Witch — all bundled up in their pink raincoats. The parrot was there, too, as the bird refused to be left behind.

They had not advanced far into the deep fog when they were halted by a queer barrier consisting of a long line of gigantic frogs, crouching so close together that no Pinkie could squeeze between them. As the heads of the frogs were turned the other way, toward the Blue Country, the army could not at first imagine what the barrier was; but Rosalie said to them:

"Our friends the frogs have agreed to help us through the Fog Bank. Climb upon their backs — as many on each frog as are able to hold on — and then we shall make the journey more quickly."

Obeying this injunction, the Pinkies began climbing upon the frogs, and by crowding close together all were able to find places. On the back of the King Frog rode Trot and her parrot, besides Rosalie, Button-Bright, Cap'n Bill and the captains of the two companies of the army.

When all were seated, clinging to one another so they would not slide off, Cap'n Bill gave the word of command and away leaped the frogs, all together. They bounded a long distance at this jump — some farther than others — and as soon as they landed they jumped again, without giving their passengers a chance to get their breaths. It was a bewildering and exciting ride, but a dozen of the huge jumps accomplished the journey and at the edge of Fog Bank each frog stopped so suddenly that the Pinkies went flying over their heads to tumble into the blue fields of the Blue Country, where they rolled in a confused mass until they could recover and scramble to their feet. No one was hurt, however, and the King Frog had been wise enough to treat his passengers more gently by slowing down at the edge and allowing his riders to slip to the ground very comfortably.

Cap'n Bill at once formed his army into line of battle and had them all remove the cumbersome raincoats, which they piled in a heap at the edge of the Fog Bank. It was a

splendid array of warriors and from where they stood they could discover several Blueskins rushing in a panic toward the Blue City, as fast as their long blue legs could carry them.

"Well, they know we're here, anyhow," said Cap'n Bill, "and instead of waitin' to see what'll they do I guess we'll jus' march on the City an' ask 'em to please surrender."

So he raised the long sharp stick with which he had armed himself and shouted:

"For-rerd—march!"

"For-ward—march!" repeated Coralie to the Sunset Tribe.

"For-ward—march!" roared Tintint to the Sunrise people.

"March—April—June—October!" screamed the parrot.

Then the drums beat and the band played and away marched the Pinkies to capture the Blue City.

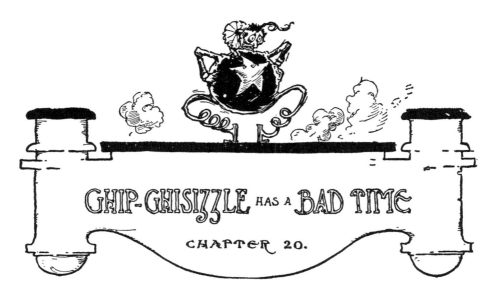

GHIP-GHISIZZLE HAS A BAD TIME

CHAPTER 20.

THE Boolooroo was quite busy at the time the Pinkies invaded his country. He had discovered the loss of the Book of Records and after being frightened 'most to death at the prospect of his fraud on the people's being made public, he decided to act boldly and hold his position as Boolooroo at any cost.

Since Ghip-Ghisizzle was to be the next Boolooroo, the king suspected him first of all, so he had the Majordomo bound with cords and brought before him, when he accused him of stealing the Book of Records. Of course Ghip-Ghisizzle denied taking the Book, but he became almost as nervous at its loss as had the Boolooroo. He secretly believed that Button-Bright had taken the Book from the Treasure Chamber, and if this were true it might prove as great a misfortune as if the king had kept it locked up. For Button-Bright had escaped into the Fog Bank and Ghip-

Ghisizzle was afraid the boy would never again be seen in the Blue Country.

He did not tell the Boolooroo of this suspicion, because in that case the king would realize he was secure, and that his deception could never be proved against him. The Majordomo simply denied taking the Record Book, and the Boolooroo did not believe he spoke truly. To prevent his rival from ever becoming the Ruler of the Blue Country the Boolooroo determined to have him patched, but for some time he could find no other Blueskin to patch him with. No one had disobeyed a command or done anything wrong, so the king was in a quandary until he discovered that a servant named Tiggle had mixed the royal nectar for Cap'n Bill, who had been ordered to do it at the time of his capture. This was sufficient excuse for the Boolooroo, who at once had Tiggle made a prisoner and brought before him.

This servant was not so long-legged as Ghip-Ghisizzle and his head was thicker and his nose flatter. But that pleased the Boolooroo all the more. He realized that when the great knife had sliced the prisoners in two, and their halves were patched together, they would present a ridiculous sight and all the Blueskins would laugh at them and avoid them. So, on the very morning that the Pinkies arrived, the Boolooroo had ordered his two prisoners brought into the room of the palace where the Great Knife stood and his soldiers were getting ready to perform the operation of patching Ghip-Ghisizzle with Tiggle, when a messenger came running to say that a great army of the Pinkies had broken through the Fog Bank.

"Never mind," said the Boolooroo, "I'll attend to them in a minute. I'm busy now."

"They are marching on the City," said the frightened messenger. "If you delay, Most High and Mighty One, we shall all be captured. You'd better save your City first and do your patching afterward."

"What!" roared the Boolooroo, "dare you dictate to me?" But he was impressed by the man's logic. After locking the prisoners, who were still bound, in the Room of the Great Knife, the Ruler hurried away to assemble his soldiers.

By this time the Pinkies had advanced halfway to the walls of the City, so the first thing the Boolooroo did was to order all the gates closed and locked and then he placed a line of soldiers on the wall to prevent any of the Pinkies from climbing over.

Therefore when Cap'n Bill's army reached the wall he was obliged to halt his ranks until he could find a way to enter the City.

Now when the Boolooroo looked through the blue-steel bars of the main gate and saw the enemy armed with sharp-pointed sticks, he began to tremble; and when he thought how painful it would be to have his body and arms and legs prodded and pricked by such weapons he groaned aloud and was very miserable. But the thought occurred to him that if he could avoid being caught by the Pinkies they would be unable to harm him. So he went among his people and reminded them how horrible it would feel to be punched full of holes by the invaders, and urged them to fight desperately and drive the Pinkies back into the Fog Bank.

Only a few of the Blueskins were soldiers, and these all belonged to the King's bodyguard, but the citizens realized they must indeed fight bravely to save themselves from getting hurt, so they promised the Boolooroo to do all they could. They armed themselves with long cords having weights fastened to the ends, and practiced throwing these weights in such a manner that the cords would wind around their enemies. Also they assembled in the streets in small groups and told each other in frightened whispers that all their trouble was due to the Boolooroo's cruel treatment of the Earth people. If he had received them as friends instead of making them slaves, they would never have escaped to the Pinkies and brought an army into the Blue Country, that they might be revenged. The Blueskins had not liked their Boolooroo, before this, and now they began to hate him, forgetting they had also treated the strangers in a very disagreeable manner.

Meantime the Six Snubnosed Princesses had seen from their rooms in a tower of the palace the army of the Pinkies marching upon them, and the sight had served to excite them greatly. They had been quarreling bitterly among themselves all the morning, and strangely enough this quarrel was all about which of them should marry Ghip-Ghisizzle. They knew that some day the Majordomo would become Boolooroo, and each one of the six had determined to marry him so as to be the Queen—and thus force her sisters to obey her commands. They paid no attention to the fact that Ghip-Ghisizzle did not want to marry any of them, for they had determined that when it was agreed who should have him they would ask their father to force the man to marry.

While they quarreled in one room of the palace Ghip-Ghisizzle was in danger of being patched in another room; but the Six Snubnosed Princesses did not know that. The arrival of the Pinkies gave them something new to talk about, so they hurried downstairs and along the corridors so as to gain the courtyard and take part in the exciting scenes.

But as they passed the closed door of the Room of the Great Knife they heard a low moan and stopped to listen. The moan was repeated and, being curious, they unlocked the door—the key having been left on the outside—and entered the room.

At once the Pinkies were forgotten, for there upon the floor, tightly bound, lay Ghip-Ghisizzle, and beside him poor Tiggle, who had uttered the moans.

Sky Island

The six Princesses sat down in a circle facing the captives and Cerulia said:

"Ghip, my dear, we will release you on one condition: That you choose a wife from among us and promise to marry the one selected, as soon as the Pinkies are driven back into the Fog Bank."

Ghip-Ghisizzle managed to shake his head. Then he said:

"Really, ladies, you must excuse me. I'd rather be patched than mismatched, as I would be with a lovely snub-nosed wife. You are too beautiful for me; go seek your husbands elsewhere."

"Monster!" cried Indigo; "if you choose me I'll scratch your eyes out!"

"If you choose me," said Cobalt, in a rage, "I'll tear out your hair by the roots!"

"If I am to be your wife," screamed Azure. "I'll mark your obstinate face with my finger nails!"

"And I," said Turquoise, passionately, "will pound your head with a broomstick!"

"I'll shake him till his teeth rattle!" shrieked Sapphire.

"The best way to manage a husband," observed Cerulia angrily, "is to pull his nose."

"Ladies," said Ghip-Ghisizzle, when he had a chance to speak, "do not anticipate these pleasures, I beg of you, for I shall choose none among you for a wife."

"We'll see about that," said Indigo.

"I think you will soon change your mind," added Azure.

"I'm going to be patched to Tiggle, here, as soon as the Boolooroo returns," said Ghip-Ghisizzle, "and it's against the law for a patched man to marry anyone. It's regarded as half-bigamy."

"Dear me!" cried Cobalt; "if he's patched he never can be Boolooroo."

"Then he mustn't be patched," declared Sapphire. "We must save him from that fate, girls, and force him to decide among us. Otherwise, none of us can ever be the Queen."

Sky Island

This being evident, they proceeded to unbind the long legs of Ghip-Ghisizzle, leaving his body and arms, however, tied fast together. Then between them they got him upon his feet and led him away, paying no attention to poor Tiggle, who whined to be released so he could fight in the war.

After a hurried consultation the Six Snubnosed Princesses decided to hide the Majordomo in one of their boudoirs, so they dragged him up the stairs to their reception room and fell to quarreling as to whose boudoir should be occupied by their captive. Not being able to settle the question they finally locked him up in a vacant room across the hall and told him he must stay there until he had decided to marry one of the Princesses and could make a choice among them.

THE CAPTURE OF CAP'N BILL

CHAPTER 21.

WHILE this was transpiring in the palace Cap'n Bill and the Pinkies had encamped before the principal gate of the City and a tent had been pitched for Trot and Button-Bright and Rosalie. The army had been very fearful and weak-kneed when it first entered the Blue Country, but perceiving that the Boolooroo and his people were afraid of them and had locked themselves up in the City, the Pinkies grew bolder and longed to make an attack.

One of them, in his curiosity to examine the Blue City, got a little too near the wall, and a blue soldier throw his cord-and-weight at him. The cord didn't wind around the Pinkie, as he was too far off, but the weight hit him in the eye and made him howl lustily as he trotted back to his comrades at full speed. After this experience the invaders were careful to keep a safe distance from the wall.

Sky Island

The Boolooroo, having made all preparations to receive the enemy, was annoyed because they held back. He was himself so nervous and excited that he became desperate and after an hour of tedious waiting, during which time he pranced around impatiently, he decided to attack the hated Pinkies and rid the country of them.

"Their dreadful color makes me hysterical," he said to his soldiers, "so if I am to have any peace of mind we must charge the foe and drive them back into the Fog Bank. But take all the prisoners you can, my brave men, and to-morrow we will have a jolly time patching them. Don't be afraid; those pink creatures have no blue blood in their veins and they'll run like rabbits when they see us coming."

Then he ordered the gate thrown open and immediately the Blueskins poured out into the open plain and began to run toward the Pinkies. The Boolooroo went out, too, but he kept well behind his people, remembering the sharp sticks with which the enemy were armed.

Cap'n Bill was alert and had told his army what to do in case of an attack. The Pinkies did not run like rabbits, but formed a solid line and knelt down with their long, sharp sticks pointed directly toward the Blueskins, the other ends being set firmly upon the ground. Of course the Blueskins couldn't run against these sharp points, so they halted a few feet away and began to swing their cord-and-weights. But the Pinkies were too close together to be caught in this manner, and now by command of Cap'n Bill they suddenly rose to their feet and began jabbing their sticks at the foe. The Blueskins hesitated until a few got pricked and began to yell with terror, when the whole of the Boolooroo's attacking party turned and ran back to the gate, their Ruler reaching it first of all. The Pinkies tried to chase them, but their round, fat legs were no match for the long, thin legs of the Blueskins, who quickly gained the gate and shut themselves up in the City again.

"It is evident," panted the Boolooroo, facing his defeated soldiers wrathfully, "that you are a pack of cowards!"

"We but followed your own royal example in running," replied the Captain.

"I merely ran back to the City to get a drink of water, for I was thirsty," declared the Boolooroo.

"So did we! So did we!" cried the soldiers, eagerly. "We were all thirsty."

"Your High and Mighty Spry and Flighty Majesty," remarked the Captain, respectfully, "it occurs to me that the weapons of the Pinkies are superior to our own. What we need, in order to oppose them successfully, is a number of sharp sticks which are longer than their own."

"True—true!" exclaimed the Boolooroo, enthusiastically. "Get to work at once and make yourselves long sharp sticks, and then we will attack the enemy again."

So the soldiers and citizens all set to work preparing long sharp sticks, and while they were doing this Rosalie the Witch had a vision in which she saw exactly what was going on inside the City wall. Queen Trot and Cap'n Bill and Button-Bright saw the vision, too, for they were all in the tent together, and the sight made them anxious.

"What can be done?" asked the girl. "The Blueskins are bigger and stronger than the Pinkies, and if they have sharp sticks which are longer than ours they will surely defeat us."

"I have one magic charm," said Rosalie, thoughtfully, "that will save our army; but I am allowed to work only one magic charm every three days—not oftener—and perhaps I'll need the magic for other things."

"Strikes me, ma'am," returned the sailor, "that what we need most on this expedition is to capture the Blueskins. If we don't, we'll need plenty of magic to help us back to the Pink Country; but if we do, we can take care of ourselves without magic."

"Very well," replied Rosalie; "I will take your advice, Cap'n, and enchant the weapons of the Pinkies."

She then went out and had all the Pinkies come before her, one by one, and she enchanted their sharp sticks by muttering some cabalistic words and making queer passes with her hands over the weapons.

Chapter Twenty-One

"Now," she said to them, "you will be powerful enough to defeat the Blueskins, whatever they may do."

The Pinkies were overjoyed at this promise and it made them very brave indeed, since they now believed they would surely be victorious.

When the Boolooroo's people were armed with long, thin lances of bluewood, all sharpened to fine points at one end, they prepared to march once more against the invaders. Their sticks were twice as long as those of the Pinkies and the Boolooroo chuckled with glee to think what fun they would have in punching holes in the round, fat bodies of his enemies.

Out from the gate they marched very boldly and pressed on to attack the Pinkies, who were drawn up in line of battle to receive them, with Cap'n Bill at their head. When the opposing forces came together, however, and the Blueskins pushed their points against the Pinkies, the weapons which had ben enchanted by Rosalie began to whirl in swift circles — so swift that the eye could scarcely follow the motion. The result was that the lances of the Boolooroo's people could not touch the Pinkies, but were thrust aside with violence and either broken in two or sent hurling through the air in all directions. Finding themselves so suddenly disarmed, the amazed Blueskins turned about and ran again, while Cap'n Bill, greatly excited by his victory, shouted to his followers to pursue the enemy, and hobbled after them as fast as he could make his wooden leg go, swinging his sharp stick as he advanced.

The Blues were in such a frightened, confused mass that they got in one another's way and could not make very good progress on the retreat, so the old sailor soon caught up with them and began jabbing at the crowd with his stick. Unfortunately the Pinkies had not followed their commander, being for the moment dazed by their success, so that Cap'n Bill was all alone among the Blueskins when he stepped his wooden leg into a hole in the ground and tumbled full length, his sharp stick flying from his hand and pricking the Boolooroo in the leg as it fell.

At this the Ruler of the Blues stopped short in his flight to yell with terror, but seeing that only the sailorman was pursuing them and that this solitary foe had tumbled flat upon the ground, he issued a command and several of his people fell upon poor Cap'n Bill, seized him in their long arms and carried him struggling into the City, where he was fast bound.

Then a panic fell upon the Pinkies at the loss of their leader, and Trot and Button-Bright called out in vain for them to rescue Cap'n Bill. By the time the army recovered their wits and prepared to obey, it was too late. And, although Trot ran with them, in her eagerness to save her friend, the gate was found to be fast barred and she knew it was impossible for them to force an entrance into the City.

Chapter Twenty-One

So she went sorrowfully back to the camp, followed by the Pinkies, and asked Rosalie what could be done.

"I'm sure I do not know," replied the Witch. "I cannot use another magic charm until three days have expired, but if they do not harm Cap'n Bill during that time I believe I can then find a way to save him."

"Three days is a long time," remarked Trot, dismally.

"The Boolooroo may decide to patch him at once," added Button-Bright, with equal sadness, for he too mourned the sailor's loss.

"It can't be helped," replied Rosalie. "I am not a fairy, my dears, but merely a witch, and so my magic powers are limited. We can only hope that the Boolooroo won't patch Cap'n Bill for three days."

When night settled down upon the camp of the Pinkies, where many tents had now been pitched, all the invaders were filled with gloom. The band tried to enliven them by playing the "Dead March," but it was not a success. The Pinkies were despondent in spite of the fact that they had repulsed the attack of the Blues, for as yet they had not succeeded in gaining the City or finding the Magic Umbrella, and the blue dusk of this dread country — which was so different from their own land of sunsets — made them all very nervous. They saw the moon rise for the first time in their lives, and its cold, silvery radiance made them shudder and prevented them from going to sleep. Trot

tried to interest them by telling them that on the Earth the people had both the sun and the moon, and loved them both; but nevertheless it is certain that had not the terrible Fog Bank stood between them and the Pink Land most of the invading army would have promptly deserted and gone back home.

Trot couldn't sleep, either, she was so worried over Cap'n Bill. She went back to the tent where Rosalie and Button-Bright were sitting in the moonlight and asked the Witch if there was no way in which she could secretly get into the City of the Blues and search for her friend. Rosalie thought it over for some time and then replied:

"We can make a rope ladder that will enable you to climb to the top of the wall, and then you can lower it to the other side and descend into the City. But, if anyone should see you, you would be captured."

"I'll risk that," said the child, excited at the prospect of gaining the side of Cap'n Bill in this adventurous way. "Please make the rope ladder at once, Rosalie!"

So the Witch took some ropes and knotted together a ladder long enough to reach to the top of the wall. When it was finished, the three — Rosalie, Trot and Button-Bright — stole out into the moonlight and crept unobserved into the shadow of the wall. The Blueskins were not keeping a very close watch, as they were confident the Pinkies could not get into the City.

Chapter Twenty-One

The hardest part of Rosalie's task was to toss up one end of the rope ladder until it would catch on some projection on top of the wall. There were few such projections, but after creeping along the wall for a distance they saw the end of a broken flagstaff near the top edge. The Witch tossed up the ladder, trying to catch it upon this point, and on the seventh attempt she succeeded.

"Good!" cried Trot; "now I can climb up."

"Don't you want me to go with you?" asked Button-Bright, a little wistfully.

"No," said the girl; "you must stay to lead the army. And, if you can think of a way, you must try to rescue us. Perhaps I'll be able to save Cap'n Bill myself; but if I don't it's all up to you, Button-Bright."

"I'll do my best," he promised.

"And here—keep my polly till I come back," added Trot, giving him the bird. "I can't take it with me, for it would be a bother, an' if it tried to spout po'try I'd be discovered in a jiffy."

As the beautiful Witch kissed the little girl good-bye she slipped upon her finger a curious ring. At once Button-Bright exclaimed:

"Why, where has she gone?"

"I'm right here," said Trot's voice by his side. "Can't you see me?"

"No," replied the boy, mystified.

Sky Island

Rosalie laughed. "It's a magic ring I've loaned you, my dear," said she, "and as long as you wear it you will be invisible to all eyes—those of Blueskins and Pinkies alike. I'm going to let you wear this wonderful ring, for it will save you from being discovered by your enemies. If at any time you wish to be seen, take the ring from your finger; but as long as you wear it, no one can see you—not even Earth people."

"Oh, thank you!" cried Trot. "That will be fine."

"I see you have another ring on your hand," said Rosalie, "and I perceive it is enchanted in some way. Where did you get it?"

"The Queen of the Mermaids gave it to me," answered Trot; "but Sky Island is so far away from the sea that the ring won't do me any good while I'm here. "It's only to call the mermaids to me if I need them, and they can't swim in the sky, you see."

Rosalie smiled and kissed her again. "Be brave, my dear," she said, "and I am sure you will be able to find Cap'n Bill without getting in danger yourself. But be careful not to let any Blueskin touch you, for while you are in contact with any person you will become visible. Keep out of their way and you will be perfectly safe. Don't lose the ring, for you must give it back to me when you return. It is one of my witchcraft treasures and I need it in my business."

Chapter Twenty-One

Then Trot climbed the ladder, although neither Button-Bright nor Rosalie could see her do so, and when she was on top the broad wall she pulled up the knotted ropes and began to search for a place to let it down on the other side. A little way off she found a bluestone seat, near to the inner edge, and attaching the ladder to this she easily descended it and found herself in the Blue City. A guard was pacing up and down near her, but as he could not see the girl he of course paid no attention to her. So, after marking the place where the ladder hung, that she might know how to reach it again, Trot hurried away through the streets of the city.

TROT'S INVISIBLE ADVENTURE

CHAPTER 22.

ALL the Blueskins except a few sentries had gone to bed and were sound asleep. A blue gloom hung over the City, which was scarcely relieved by a few bluish, wavering lights here and there, but Trot knew the general direction in which the palace lay and she decided to go there first. She believed the Boolooroo would surely keep so important a prisoner as Cap'n Bill locked up in his own palace.

Once or twice the little girl lost her way, for the streets were very puzzling to one not accustomed to them, but finally she sighted the great palace and went up to the entrance. There she found a double guard posted. They were sitting on a bench outside the doorway and both stood up as she approached.

"We thought we heard footsteps," said one.

"So did we," replied the other; "yet there is no one in sight."

Chapter Twenty-Two

Trot then saw that the guards were the two patched men, Jimfred Jonesjinks and Fredjim Jinksjones, who had been talking together quite cheerfully. It was the first time the girl had seen them together and she marveled at the queer patching that had so strongly united them, yet so thoroughly separated them.

"You see," remarked Jimfred, as they seated themselves again upon the bench, "the Boolooroo has ordered the patching to take place to-morrow morning after breakfast. The old Earth man is to be patched to poor Tiggle, instead of Ghip-Ghisizzle, who has in some way managed to escape from the Room of the Great Knife — no one knows how but Tiggle, and Tiggle won't tell."

"We're sorry for anyone who has to be patched," replied Fredjim in a reflective tone, "for although it didn't hurt us as much as we expected, it's a terrible mix-up to be in — until we become used to our strange combination. You and we are about alike now, Jimfred, although we were so different before."

"Not so," said Jimfred; "we are really more intelligent than you are, for the left side of our brain was always the keenest before we were patched."

"That may be," admitted Fredjim, "but we are much the strongest, because our right arm was by far the best before we were patched."

"We are not sure of that," responded Jimfred, "for we have a right arm, too, and it is pretty strong."

"We will test it," suggested the other, "by all pulling upon one end of this bench with our right arms. Whichever can pull the bench from the others must be the stronger."

While they were tussling at the bench, dragging it first here and then there in the trial of strength, Trot opened the door of the palace and walked in. It was pretty dark in the hall and only a few dim blue lights showed at intervals down the long corridors. As the girl walked through these passages she could hear snores of various degrees coming from behind some of the closed doors and knew that all the regular inmates of the place were sound asleep. So she mounted to the upper floor, and thinking she would be likely to find Cap'n Bill in the Room of the Great Knife she went there and tried the door. It was locked, but the key had been left on the outside. She waited until the sentry who was pacing the corridor had his back toward her and then she turned the key and slipped within, softly closing the door behind her.

It was dark as pitch in the room and Trot didn't know how to make a light. After a moment's thought she began feeling her way to the window, stumbling over objects as she went. Every time she made a noise some one groaned, and that made the child uneasy.

At last she found a window and managed to open the

shutters and let the moonlight in. It wasn't a very strong moonlight but it enabled her to examine the interior of the room. In the center stood the Great Knife which the Boolooroo used to split people in two when he patched them, and at one side was a dark form huddled upon the floor and securely bound.

Trot hastened to this form and knelt beside it, but was disappointed to find it was only Tiggle. The man stirred a little and rolled against Trot's knee, when she at once became visible to him.

"Oh, it's the Earth Child," said he. "Are you condemned to be patched, too, little one?"

"No," answered Trot. "Tell me where Cap'n Bill is."

"I can't," said Tiggle. "The Boolooroo has hidden him until to-morrow morning, when he's to be patched to me. Ghip-Ghisizzle was to have been my mate, but Ghip escaped, being carried away by the Six Snubnosed Princesses."

"Why?" she asked.

"One of them means to marry him," explained Tiggle.

"Oh, that's worse than being patched!" cried Trot.

"Much worse," said Tiggle, with a groan.

But now an idea occurred to the girl.

"Would you like to escape?" she asked the captive.

"I would, indeed!" said he.

"If I get you out of the palace, can you hide yourself so that you won't be found?"

"Certainly!" he declared. "I know a house where I can hide so snugly that all the Boolooroo's soldiers cannot find me."

"All right," said Trot; "I'll do it; for when you're gone the Boolooroo will have no one to patch Cap'n Bill to."

"He may find some one else," suggested the prisoner.

"But it will take him time to do that, and time is all I want," answered the child. Even while she spoke Trot was busy with the knots in the cords, and presently she had unbound Tiggle, who soon got upon his feet.

"Now, I'll go to one end of the passage and make a noise," said she; "and when the guard runs to see what it is you must run the other way. Outside the palace Jimfred and Fredjim are on guard, but if you tip over the bench they are seated on you can easily escape them."

"I'll do that, all right," promised the delighted Tiggle. "You've made a friend of me, little girl, and if ever I can help you I'll do it with pleasure."

Then Trot started for the door and Tiggle could no longer see her because she was not now touching him. The man was much surprised at her disappearance, but listened carefully and when he heard the girl make a noise at one end of the corridor he opened the door and ran in the opposite direction, as he had been told to do.

Of course the guard could not discover what made the noise and Trot ran little risk, as she was careful not to let him touch her. When Tiggle had safely escaped, the little girl wandered through the palace in search of Cap'n Bill, but soon decided such a quest in the dark was likely to fail and she must wait until morning. She was tired, too, and thought she would find a vacant room—of which there were many in the big palace—and go to sleep until daylight. She remembered there was a comfortable vacant room just opposite the suite of the Six Snubnosed Princesses, so she stole softly up to it and tried the door. It was locked, but the key was outside, as the Blueskins seldom took a door-key away from its place. So she turned the key, opened the door, and walked in.

Now, this was the chamber in which Ghip-Ghisizzle had been confined by the Princesses, his arms being bound tight to his body but his legs left free. The Boolooroo in his search had failed to discover what had become of Ghip-Ghisizzle, but the poor man had been worried every minute for fear his retreat would be discovered or that the terrible Princesses would come for him and nag him until he went crazy. There was one window in his room and the prisoner had managed to push open the sash with his knees. Looking out, he found that a few feet below the window was the broad wall that ran all around the palace gardens. A little way to the right the wall joined the wall of the City, being on the same level with it.

Ghip-Ghisizzle had been thinking deeply upon this discovery, and he decided that if anyone entered his room he would get through the window, leap down upon the wall and try in this way to escape. It would be a dangerous leap, for as his arms were bound he might topple off the wall into the garden; but he resolved to take this chance.

Therefore, when Trot rattled at the door of his room Ghip-Ghisizzle ran and seated himself upon the window-sill, dangling his long legs over the edge. When she finally opened the door he slipped off and let himself fall to the wall, where he doubled up in a heap. The next minute, however, he had scrambled to his feet and was running swiftly along the garden wall.

Trot, finding the window open, came and looked out, and she saw the Majordomo's tall form hastening along the top of the wall. The guards saw him, too, outlined against the sky in the moonlight, and they began yelling at him to stop; but Ghip-Ghisizzle kept right on until he reached the City Wall, when he began to follow that. More guards were yelling, now, running along the foot of the wall to keep the fugitive in sight, and people began to pour out of the houses and join in the chase.

Poor Ghip realized that if he kept on the wall he would merely circle the city and finally be caught. If he leaped down into the City he would be seized at once. Just then he came opposite the camp of the Pinkies and decided to trust himself to the mercies of his Earth friends rather than

Chapter Twenty-Two

be made a prisoner by his own people, who would obey the commands of their detested but greatly feared Boolooroo. So, suddenly he gave a mighty leap and came down into the field outside the City. Again he fell in a heap and rolled over and over, for it was a high wall and the jump a dangerous one; but finally he recovered and got upon his feet, delighted to find he had broken none of his bones.

Some of the Blueskins had by now opened a gate, and out rushed a crowd to capture the fugitive; but Ghip-Ghisizzle made straight for the camp of the Pinkies and his pursuers did not dare follow him far in that direction. They soon gave up the chase and returned to the City, while the runaway Majordomo was captured by Captain Coralie and marched away to the tent of Rosalie the Witch, a prisoner of the Pinkies.

THE GIRL AND THE BOOLOOROO

CHAPTER 23.

TROT watched from the window the escape of Ghip-Ghisizzle but did not know, of course, who it was. Then, after the City had quieted down again, she lay upon the bed without undressing and was sound asleep in a minute.

The blue dawn was just breaking when she opened her eyes with a start of fear that she might have overslept, but soon she found that no one else in the palace was yet astir. Even the guards had gone to sleep by this time and were adding their snores to the snores of the other inhabitants of the Royal Palace. So the little girl got up and, finding a ewer of water and a basin upon the dresser, washed herself carefully and then looked in a big mirror to see how her hair was. To her astonishment there was no reflection at all; the mirror was blank so far as Trot was concerned. She laughed a little, at that, remembering she wore the ring of

Chapter Twenty-Three

Rosalie the Witch, which rendered her invisible. Then she slipped quietly out of the room and found it was already light enough in the corridors for her to see all objects distinctly.

After hesitating a moment which way to turn she decided to visit the Snubnosed Princesses and passed through the big reception room to the sleeping room of Indigo. There this Princess, the crossest and most disagreeable of all the disagreeable six, was curled up in bed and slumbering cosily. The little blue dog came trotting out of Indigo's boudoir and crowed like a rooster, for although he could not see Trot his keen little nose scented her presence. Thinking it time the Princess awoke, Trot leaned over and gave her snubnose a good tweak, and at once Indigo yelled like an Indian and sat up, glaring around her to see who had dared to pull her nose. Trot, standing back in the room, threw a sofa pillow that caught the Princess on the side of her head. At once Indigo sprang out of bed and rushed into the chamber of Cobalt, which adjoined her own. Thinking it was this sister who had slyly attacked her, Indigo rushed at the sleeping Cobalt and slapped her face.

At once there was war. The other four Princesses, hearing the screams and cries of rage, came running into Cobalt's room and as fast as they appeared Trot threw pillows at them, so that presently all six were indulging in a free-for-all battle and snarling like tigers.

223

Sky Island

The blue lamb came trotting into the room and Trot leaned over and patted the pretty little animal; but as she did so she became visible for an instant, each pat destroying the charm of the ring while the girl was in contact with a living creature. These flashes permitted some of the Princesses to see her and at once they rushed toward her with furious cries. But the girl realized what had happened, and leaving the lamb she stepped back into a corner and her frenzied enemies failed to find her. It was a little dangerous, though, remaining in a room where six girls were feeling all around for her, so she went away and left them to their vain search while she renewed her hunt for Cap'n Bill.

The sailorman did not seem to be in any of the rooms she entered, so she decided to visit the Boolooroo's own apartments. In the room where Rosalie's vision had shown them the Magic Umbrella lying under a cabinet, Trot attempted to find it, for she considered that next to rescuing Cap'n Bill this was the most important task to accomplish; but the umbrella had been taken away and was no longer beneath the cabinet. This was a severe disappointment to the child, but she reflected that the umbrella was surely some place in the Blue City, so there was no need to despair.

Finally she entered the King's own sleeping chamber and found the Boolooroo in bed and asleep, with a funny night-cap tied over his egg-shaped head. As Trot looked at him she was surprised to see that he had one foot out of bed and

224

that to his big toe was tied a cord that led out of the bed-chamber into a small dressing room beyond. Trot slowly followed this cord and in the dressing room came upon Cap'n Bill, who was lying asleep upon a lounge and snoring with great vigor. His arms were tied to his body and his body was tied fast to the lounge. The wooden leg stuck out into the room at an angle and the shoe on his one foot had been removed so that the end of the cord could be fastened to the sailor's big toe.

This arrangement had been a clever thought of the Boolooroo. Fearing his important prisoner might escape before he was patched, as Ghip-Ghisizzle had done, the cruel King of the Blues had kept Cap'n Bill in his private apartments and had tied his own big toe to the prisoner's big toe, so that if the sailor made any attempt to get away he would pull on the cord, and that would arouse the Boolooroo.

Trot saw through this cunning scheme at once, so the first thing she did was to untie the cord from Cap'n Bill's big toe and retie it to a leg of the lounge. Then she unfastened her friend's bonds and leaned over to give his leathery face a smacking kiss.

Cap'n Bill sat up and rubbed his eyes. He looked around the room and rubbed his eyes again, seeing no one who could have kissed him. Then he discovered that his bonds had been removed and he rubbed his eyes once more to make sure he was not dreaming.

The little girl laughed softly.

"Trot!" exclaimed the sailor, recognizing her voice.

Then Trot came up and took his hand, the touch at once rendering her visible to him.

"Dear me!" said the bewildered sailor; "however did you get here, mate, in the Boolooroo's own den? Is the Blue City captured?"

"Not yet," she replied; "but *you* are, Cap'n, and I've come to save you."

"All alone, Trot?"

"All alone, Cap'n Bill. But it's got to be done, jus' the same." And then she explained about the magic ring Rosalie had lent her, which rendered her invisible while she wore it—unless she touched some living creature. Cap'n Bill was much interested.

"I'm willing to be saved, mate," he said, "for the Boo-l'roo is set on patchin' me right after breakfas', which I hope the cook'll be late with."

"Who are you to be patched with?" she asked.

"A feller named Tiggle, who's in disgrace 'cause he mixed the royal necktie for me."

"That was nectar—not necktie," corrected Trot. "But you needn't be 'fraid of bein' patched with Tiggle, 'cause I've set him loose. By this time he's in hiding, where he can't be found."

"That's good," said Cap'n Bill, nodding approval; "but

Chapter Twenty-Three

the blamed ol' Bool'roo's sure to find some one else. What's to be done, mate?"

Trot thought about it for a moment. Then she remembered how some unknown man had escaped from the palace the night before, by means of the wall, which he had reached from the window of the very chamber in which she had slept. Cap'n Bill might easily do the same. And the rope ladder she had used would help the sailor down from the top of the wall.

"Could you climb down a rope ladder, Cap'n?" she asked.

"Like enough," said he. "I've done it many a time on shipboard."

"But you hadn't a wooden leg then," she reminded him.

"The wooden leg won't bother much," he assured her.

So Trot tied a small sofa cushion around the end of his wooden leg, so it wouldn't make any noise pounding upon the floor, and then she quietly led the sailor through the room of the sleeping Boolooroo and through several other rooms until they came to the passage. Here a soldier was on guard, but he had fallen asleep for a moment, in order to rest himself. They passed this Blueskin without disturbing him and soon reached the chamber opposite the suite of the Six Snub-nosed Princesses, whom they could hear still quarreling loudly among themselves.

Trot locked the door from the inside, so no one could disturb them, and then led the sailor to the window. The garden was just below.

"But—good gracious me! It's a drop o' ten feet, Trot," he exclaimed.

"And you've only one foot to drop, Cap'n," she said, laughing. "Couldn't you let yourself down with one of the sheets from the bed?"

"I'll try," he rejoined. "But, can *you* do that circus act, Trot?"

"Oh, I'm goin' to stay here an' find the Magic Umbrella," she replied. "Bein' invis'ble, Cap'n, I'm safe enough. What I want to do is to see you safe back with the Pinkies, an' then I'll manage to hold my own all right, never fear."

So they brought a blue sheet and tied one end to a post of the blue bed and let the other end dangle out the blue window.

"Good-bye, mate," said Cap'n Bill, preparing to descend; "don't get reckless."

"I won't, Cap'n. Don't worry."

Then he grasped the sheet with both hands and easily let himself down to the wall. Trot had told him where to find the rope ladder she had left and how to fasten it to the broken flagstaff so he could climb down into the field outside the City.

As soon as he was safe on the wall Cap'n Bill began to hobble along the broad top toward the connecting wall that surrounded the entire City—just as Ghip-Ghisizzle had done—and Trot anxiously watched him from the window.

But the Blue City was now beginning to waken to life. One of the soldiers came from a house, sleepily yawning and stretching himself, and presently his eyes lit upon the huge form of Cap'n Bill hastening along the top of the wall. The soldier gave a yell that aroused a score of his comrades and brought them tumbling into the street. When they saw how the Boolooroo's precious prisoner was escaping they instantly became alert and wide-awake, and every one started in pursuit along the foot of the wall.

Of course the long-legged Blueskins could run faster than poor Cap'n Bill. Some of them soon got ahead of the old sailorman and came to the rope ladder which Trot had left dangling from the stone bench, where it hung down inside the City. The Blue soldiers promptly mounted this ladder and so gained the wall, heading off the fugitive. When Cap'n Bill came up, panting and all out of breath, the Blueskins seized him and held him fast.

Cap'n Bill was terribly disappointed at being recaptured, and so was Trot, who had eagerly followed his every movement from her window in the palace. The little girl could have cried with vexation, and I think she did weep a few tears before she recovered her courage; but Cap'n Bill was a philosopher, in his way, and had learned to accept ill fortune cheerfully. Knowing he was helpless, he made no protest when they again bound him and carried him down the ladder like a bale of goods.

Others were also disappointed by his capture. Button-Bright had heard the parrot squawking:

"Oh, there's Cap'n Bill! There's Cap'n Bill!
I see him still — up on that hill!
It's Cap'n Bill!"

So the boy ran out of his tent to find the sailor hurrying along the top of the wall as fast as he could go. At once Button-Bright aroused Coralie, who got her Pinkies together and quickly marched them toward the wall to assist in the escape of her Commander in Chief.

But they were too late. Before they could reach the wall the Blueskins had captured Trot's old friend and lugged him down into the City, so Coralie and Button-Bright were forced to return to their camp discomfited. There Ghip-Ghisizzle and Rosalie were awaiting them and they all went into the Witch's tent and held a council of war.

"Tell me," said Ghip-Ghisizzle to Button-Bright, "did you not take the Royal Record Book from the Treasure Chamber of the Boolooroo?"

"I did," replied the boy. "I remember that you wanted it and so I have kept it with me ever since that night. Here it is," and he presented the little blue book to the Majordomo, the only friend the adventurers had found among all the Blueskins.

Ghip-Ghisizzle took the book eagerly and at once began turning over its leaves.

"Ah!" he exclaimed, presently, "it is just as I suspected. The wicked Boolooroo had already reigned over the Blue Country three hundred years last Thursday, so that now he has no right to rule at all. I, myself, have been the rightful Ruler of the Blues since Thursday, and yet this cruel and deceitful man has not only deprived me of my right to succeed him, but he has tried to have me patched, so that I could never become the Boolooroo."

"Does the book tell how old he is?" asked Button-Bright.

"Yes; he is now five hundred years old, and has yet another hundred years to live. He planned to rule the Blue Country until the last, but I now know the deception he has practiced and have the Royal Record Book to prove it. With this I shall be able to force him to resign, that I may take his place, for all the people will support me and abide by the Law. The tyrant will perhaps fight me and my cause desperately, but I am sure to win in the end."

"If we can help you," said Button-Bright, "the whole Pink Army will fight for you. Only, if you win, you must promise to give me back my Magic Umbrella and let us fly away to our own homes again."

"I will do that most willingly," agreed Ghip-Ghisizzle.

"And now let us consult together how best to take the Blue City and capture the Boolooroo. As I know my own country much better than you or the Pinkies do, I think I can find a way to accomplish our purpose."

THE AMAZING CONQUEST OF THE BLUES

CHAPTER 24.

THE shouting and excitement in the City following upon the recapture of Cap'n Bill aroused the sleeping Boolooroo. He found the cord still tied to his big toe and at first imagined his prisoner was safe in the dressing room. While he put on his clothes the king occasionally gave the cord a sudden pull, hoping to hurt Cap'n Bill's big toe and make him yell; but as no response came to this mean action the Boolooroo finally looked into the room, only to find he had been pulling on a leg of the couch and that his prisoner had escaped.

Then he flew into a mighty rage and running out into the hall he aimed a blow at the unfaithful guard, knocking the fellow off his feet. Then he rushed down stairs into the courtyard, shouting loudly for his soldiers and threatening to patch everybody in his dominions if the sailorman was not recaptured.

Sky Island

While the Boolooroo stormed and raged a band of soldiers and citizens came marching in, surrounding Cap'n Bill, who was again firmly bound.

"So-ho!" roared the monarch, "you thought you could defy me, Earth Clod, did you? But you were mistaken. No one can resist the Mighty Boolooroo of the Blues, so it is folly for you to rebel against my commands. Hold him fast, my men, and as soon as I've had my coffee and oatmeal I'll take him to the Room of the Great Knife and patch him."

"I wouldn't mind a cup o' coffee myself," said Cap'n Bill. "I've had consid'ble exercise this mornin' and I'm all ready for breakfas'."

"Very well," replied the Boolooroo, "you shall eat with me, for then I can keep an eye on you. My guards are not to be trusted, and I don't mean to let you out of my sight again until you are patched."

So Cap'n Bill and the Boolooroo had breakfast together, six Blueskins standing in a row back of the sailorman to grab him if he attempted to escape. But Cap'n Bill made no such attempt, knowing it would be useless.

Trot was in the room, too, standing in a corner and listening to all that was said while she racked her little brain for an idea that would enable her to save Cap'n Bill from being patched. No one could see her, so no one—not even Cap'n Bill—knew she was there.

After breakfast was over a procession was formed, headed

by the Boolooroo, and they marched the prisoner through the palace until they came to the Room of the Great Knife. Invisible Trot followed soberly after them, still wondering what she could do to save her friend.

As soon as they entered the Room of the Great Knife the Boolooroo gave a yell of disappointment.

"What's become of Tiggle?" he shouted. "Where's Tiggle? Who has released Tiggle? Go at once, you dummies, and find him — or it will go hard with you!"

The frightened soldiers hurried away to find Tiggle, and Trot was well pleased because she knew Tiggle was by this time safely hidden.

The Boolooroo stamped up and down the room, muttering threats and declaring Cap'n Bill should be patched whether Tiggle was found or not, and while they waited Trot took time to make an inspection of the place, which she now saw for the first time in broad daylight.

The Room of the Great Knife was high and big, and around it ran rows of benches for the spectators to sit upon. In one place — at the head of the room — was a raised platform for the royal family, with elegant throne-chairs for the King and Queen and six smaller but richly upholstered chairs for the Snubnosed Princesses. The poor Queen, by the way, was seldom seen, as she passed all her time playing solitaire with a deck that was one card short, hoping that before she had lived her entire six hundred years she would win the game. Therefore her Majesty paid no attention to anyone and no one paid any attention to her.

In the center of the room stood the terrible knife that gave the place its name — a name dreaded by every inhabitant of the Blue City. The knife was built into a huge framework, like a derrick, that reached to the ceiling, and it was so arranged that when the Boolooroo pulled a cord the great blade would drop down in its frame and neatly cut in two the person who stood under it. And, in order that the slicing would be accurate, there was another frame, to which the prisoner was tied so that he couldn't wiggle either way. This frame was on rollers, so that it could be placed directly underneath the knife.

While Trot was observing this dreadful machine the door opened and in walked the Six Snubnosed Princesses, all in a row and with their chins up, as if they disdained everyone but themselves. They were magnificently dressed and their blue hair was carefully arranged in huge towers upon their heads, with blue plumes stuck into the tops. These plumes waved gracefully in the air with every mincing step the Princesses took. Rich jewels of blue stones glittered upon their persons and the royal ladies were fully as gorgeous as they were haughty and overbearing. They marched to their chairs and seated themselves to enjoy the cruel scene their father was about to enact, and Cap'n Bill bowed to them politely and said:

Chapter Twenty-Four

"Mornin', girls; hope ye feel as well as ye look."

"Papa," exclaimed Turquoise, angrily, "can you not prevent this vile Earth Being from addressing us? It is an insult to be spoken to by one about to be patched."

"Control yourselves, my dears," replied the Boolooroo; "᠎he worst punishment I know how to inflict on anyone, this prisoner is about to suffer. You'll see a very pretty patching, my royal daughters."

"When?" inquired Cobalt.

"When? As soon as the soldiers return with Tiggle," said he.

But just then in came the soldiers to say that Tiggle could not be found anywhere in the City; he had disappeared as mysteriously as had Ghip-Ghisizzle. Immediately the Boolooroo flew into another towering rage.

"Villains!" he shouted, "go out and arrest the first living thing you meet, and whoever it proves to be will be instantly patched to Cap'n Bill."

The Captain of the Guards hesitated to obey this order.

"Suppose it's a friend?" he suggested.

"Friend!" roared the Boolooroo; "I haven't a friend in the country. Tell me, sir, do you know of anyone who is my friend?"

The Captain shook his head.

"I can't think of anyone just now, your Spry and Flighty High and Mighty Majesty," he answered.

237

"Of course not," said the Boolooroo. "Everyone hates me, and I don't object to that because I hate everybody. But I'm the Ruler here, and I'll do as I please. Go and capture the first living creature you see, and bring him here to be patched to Cap'n Bill."

So the Captain took a file of soldiers and went away very sorrowful, for he did not know who would be the victim, and if the Boolooroo had no friends, the Captain had plenty, and did not wish to see them patched.

Meantime Trot, being invisible to all, was roaming around the room and behind a bench she found a small coil of rope, which she picked up. Then she seated herself in an out-of-the-way place and quietly waited.

Suddenly there was a noise in the corridor and evidence of scuffling and struggling. Then the door flew open and in came the soldiers dragging a great blue billygoat, which was desperately striving to get free.

"Villains!" howled the Boolooroo; "what does this mean?"

"Why, you said to fetch the first living creature we met, and that was this billygoat," replied the Captain, panting hard as he held fast to one of the goat's horns.

The Boolooroo stared a moment and then he fell back in his throne, laughing boisterously. The idea of patching Cap'n Bill to a goat was vastly amusing to him, and the more he thought of it the more he roared with laughter. Some of the soldiers laughed, too, being tickled with the absurd notion, and the Six Snubnosed Princesses all sat up straight and permitted themselves to smile contemptuously. This would indeed be a severe punishment; therefore the Princesses were pleased at the thought of Cap'n Bill's becoming half a billygoat, and the billygoat's being half Cap'n. Bill.

"They look something alike, you know," suggested the Captain of the Guards, looking from one to the other doubtfully; "and they're nearly the same size if you stand the goat on his hind legs. They've both got the same style of whiskers and they're both of 'em obstinate and dangerous; so they ought to make a good patch."

"Splendid! Fine! Glorious!" cried the Boolooroo, wiping the tears of merriment from his eyes. "We will proceed with the Ceremony of Patching at once."

Cap'n Bill regarded the billygoat with distinct disfavor, and the billygoat glared evilly upon Cap'n Bill. Trot was horrified, and wrung her little hands in sore perplexity, for this was a most horrible fate that awaited her dear old friend.

"First, bind the Earth Man in the frame," commanded the Boolooroo. "We'll slice him in two before we do the same to the billygoat."

So they seized Cap'n Bill and tied him into the frame so that he couldn't move a jot in any direction. Then they rolled the frame underneath the Great Knife and handed the Boolooroo the cord that released the blade.

But while this was going on Trot had crept up and fastened one end of her rope to the frame in which Cap'n Bill was confined. Then she stood back and watched the Boolooroo, and just as he pulled the cord she pulled on her rope and dragged the frame on its rollers away, so that the Great Knife fell with a crash and sliced nothing but the air.

"Huh!" exclaimed the Boolooroo; "that's queer. Roll him up again, soldiers."

The soldiers again rolled the frame in position, having first pulled the Great Knife once more to the top of the derrick. The immense blade was so heavy that it took the strength of seven Blueskins to raise it.

When all was in readiness the King pulled the cord a second time and Trot at the same instant pulled upon her rope. The same thing happened as before. Cap'n Bill rolled away in his frame and the knife fell harmlessly.

Now, indeed, the Boolooroo was as angry as he was amazed. He jumped down from the platform and commanded the soldiers to raise the Great Knife into position. When this had been accomplished the Boolooroo leaned over to try to discover why the frame rolled away — seemingly of its own accord — and he was the more puzzled because it had never done such a thing before.

As he stood, bent nearly double, his back was toward the

Chapter Twenty-Four

billygoat, which, in their interest and excitement, the soldiers were holding in a careless manner. At once the goat gave a leap, escaped from the soldiers and with bowed head rushed upon the Boolooroo. Before any could stop him he butted his Majesty so furiously that the King soared far into the air and tumbled in a heap among the benches, where he lay moaning and groaning.

The goat's warlike spirit was roused by this successful attack. Finding himself free, he turned and assaulted the soldiers, butting them so fiercely that they tumbled down in bunches and as soon as they could rise again ran frantically from the room and along the corridors as if a fiend was after them. By this time the goat was so animated by the spirit of conquest that he rushed at the Six Snubnosed Princesses, who had all climbed upon their chairs and were screaming in a panic of fear. Six times the goat butted and each time he tipped over a chair and sent a haughty Princess groveling upon the floor, where the ladies got mixed up in their long blue trains and flounces and laces, and struggled wildly until they recovered their footing. Then they sped in great haste for the door, and the goat gave a final butt that sent the row of royal ladies all diving into the corridor in another tangle, whereupon they shrieked in a manner that terrified everyone within sound of their voices.

As the Room of the Great Knife was now cleared of all but Cap'n Bill — who was tied in his frame — and of Trot and the moaning Boolooroo, who lay hidden behind the benches, the goat gave a victorious bleat and stood in the doorway to face any enemy that might appear.

Trot had been as surprised as anyone at this sudden change of conditions, but she was quick to take advantage of the opportunities it afforded. First she ran with her rope to the goat and, as the animal could not see her, she easily succeeded in tying the rope around its horns and fastening the loose end to a pillar of the doorway. Next she hurried to Cap'n Bill and began to unbind him, and as she touched the sailor she became visible. He nodded cheerfully, then, and said:

"I had a notion it was you, mate, as saved me from the knife. But it were a pretty close call an' I hope it won't happen again. I couldn't shiver much, bein' bound so tight, but when I'm loose I mean to have jus' one good shiver to relieve my feelin's."

"Shiver all you want to, Cap'n," she said, as she removed the last bonds; "but first you've got to help me save us both."

"As how?" he asked, stepping from the frame.

"Come and get the Boolooroo," she said, going toward the benches.

The sailor followed and pulled out the Boolooroo, who, when he saw the terrible goat was captured and tied fast, quickly recovered his courage.

"Hi, there!" he cried; "where are my soldiers? What do

you mean, prisoner, by daring to lay hands upon me? Let me go this minute or I'll—I'll have you patched *twice!*"

"Don't mind him, Cap'n," said Trot, "but fetch him along to the frame."

The Boolooroo looked around to see where the voice came from and Cap'n Bill grinned joyfully and caught up the king

in both his strong arms, dragging the struggling Monarch of the Blues to the frame.

"Stop it! How dare you?" roared the frightened Boolooroo. "I'll have revenge!—I'll—I'll—"

"You'll take it easy, 'cause you can't help yourself," said Cap'n Bill. "What next, Queen Trot?"

"Hold him steady in the frame and I'll tie him up," she replied. So Cap'n Bill held the Boolooroo, and the girl tied him fast in position, as Cap'n Bill had been tied, so that his Majesty couldn't wiggle at all.

Then they rolled the frame in position underneath the Great Knife and Trot held in her hand the cord which would release it.

"All right, Cap'n," she said in a satisfied tone, "I guess we can run this Blue Country ourselves, after this."

The Boolooroo was terrified to find himself in danger of being sliced by the same knife he had so often wickedly employed to slice others. Like Cap'n Bill, he had no room to shiver, but he groaned very dismally and was so full of fear that his blue hair nearly stood on end.

THE RULER OF SKY ISLAND

CHAPTER 25.

THE girl now took off Rosalie's ring and put it carefully away in her pocket.

"It won't matter who sees me now," she remarked, "an' I want 'em to know that you an' me, Cap'n, are running this kingdom. I'm Queen o' the Pinkies an' Boolooroocss o' the Blues, an——"

"What's that?" asked the sailor. "You're — you're *what*, Trot?"

"Boolooroocss. Isn't that right, Cap'n?"

"I dunno, mate. It sounds bigger ner you are, an' I don't like the word, anyhow. S'pose you jus' call yourself the Boss? That fills the bill an' don't need pernouncin'."

"All right," she said; "Queen o' the Pinkies an' Boss o' the Blues. Seems funny, don't it, Cap'n Bill?"

Just then they heard a sound of footsteps in the corridor.

245

The soldiers had partly recovered their courage and, fearful of the anger of their dreaded Boolooroo, whom the Princesses declared would punish them severely, had ventured to return to the room. They came rather haltingly, though, and the Captain of the Guards first put his head cautiously through the doorway to see if the coast was clear. The goat discovered him and tried to make a rush, but the rope held the animal back and when the Captain saw this he came forward more boldly.

"Halt!" cried Trot.

The Captain halted, his soldiers peering curiously over his shoulders and the Six Snubnosed Princesses looking on from behind, where they considered themselves safe.

"If anyone dares enter this room without my permission," said Trot, "I'll pull this cord and slice your master that once was the Boolooroo."

"Don't come in! Don't come in!" yelled the Boolooroo in a terrified voice.

Then they saw that the sailor was free and the Boolooroo bound in his place. The soldiers were secretly glad to observe this, but the Princesses were highly indignant.

"Release his Majesty at once!" cried Indigo from the corridor. "You shall be severely punished for this rebellion."

"Don't worry," replied Trot. "His Majesty isn't his Majesty any longer; he's jus' a common Blueskin. Cap'n Bill and I perpose runnin' this Island ourselves, after this.

246

Chapter Twenty-Five

You've all got to obey *me*, for I'm the Booloorooess—no, I mean the Boss—o' the Blues, and I've a notion to run things my own way."

"You can't," said Turquoise, scornfully; "the Law says——"

"Bother the Law!" exclaimed Trot. "I'll make the Laws myself, from now on, and I'll unmake every Law you ever had before I conquered you."

"Oh. Have you conquered us, then?" asked the Captain of the Guards, in a surprised tone.

"Of course," said Trot. "Can't you see?"

"It looks like it," admitted the Captain.

"Cap'n Bill is goin' to be my General o' the Army an' the Royal Manager o' the Blue Country," continued Trot; "so you'll mind what he says."

"Nonsense!" shouted Indigo. "March in and capture them, Captain! Never mind if they do slice the Boolooroo. I'm his daughter, and *I'll* rule the kingdom."

"You won't!" screamed Cobalt. "I'll rule it!"

"I'll rule it myself!" cried Cerulia.

"No, no!" yelled Turquoise; "I'll be the Ruler."

"That shall be *my* privilege!" shouted Sapphire. Cobalt began to say:

"I'm the——"

"Be quiet!" said Trot, sternly. "Would you have your own father sliced, so that you could rule in his place?"

247

"Yes, yes; of course!" rejoined the six Princesses, without a second's hesitation.

"Well, well! What d' ye think o' that, Mr. Boolooroo?" asked Cap'n Bill.

"They're undutiful daughters; don't pay any attention to them," replied the frightened Boolooroo.

"We're not goin' to," said Trot. "Now, you Blue Cap'n, who are you and your soldiers going to obey — me or the snub-nosed ones?"

"You!" declared the Captain of the Guards, positively, for he hated the Princesses, as did all the Blueskins.

"Then escort those girls to their rooms, lock 'em in, an' put a guard before the door."

At once the soldiers seized the Princesses and, notwithstanding their snarls and struggles, marched them to their rooms and locked them in. While they were gone on this errand the Boolooroo begged to be released, whining and wailing for fear the knife would fall upon him. But Trot did not think it safe to unbind him just then. When the soldiers returned she told their leader to put a strong guard before the palace and to admit no one unless either she or Cap'n Bill gave the order to do so.

The soldiers obeyed readily, and when Trot and Cap'n Bill were left alone they turned the goat loose in the Room of the Great Knife and then locked the animal in with the Boolooroo.

Chapter Twenty-Five

"The billygoat is the very best guard we could have, for ever'body's 'fraid o' him," remarked Cap'n Bill, as he put the key of the room in his pocket. "So now, Queen Trot, what's next on the program?"

"Next," said Trot, "we're goin' to hunt for that umbrel, Cap'n. I don't mean to stay in this dismal Blue Country long, even if I am the Queen. Let's find the umbrel and get home as soon as we can."

"That suits me," the sailor joyfully exclaimed, and then the two began a careful search through the palace.

They went into every room and looked behind the furniture and underneath the beds and in every crack and corner, but no place could they spy the Magic Umbrella. Cap'n Bill even ventured to enter the rooms of the Six Snubnosed Princesses, who were by this time so thoroughly alarmed that they had become meek and mild as could be. But the umbrella wasn't there, either.

Finally they returned to the great throne room of the palace, where they seated themselves on the throne and tried to think what could possibly have become of the precious umbrella. While they were sitting and talking together the Captain of the Guards entered and bowed respectfully.

"Beg pardon, your Small-Sized Majesty," said he to Trot, "but it is my duty to report that the Pinkies are preparing to attack the City."

"Oh; I'd forgotten the Pinkies!" exclaimed the girl.

"Tell me, Captain, have you such a thing as a Brass Band in this City?"

"We have two fine bands, but they are not brass," replied the Captain. "Their instruments are made of blue metal."

"Well, order 'em out," commanded Trot. "And, say; get all the soldiers together and tell all the people there's go-

ing to be a high time in the Blue City to-night. We'll have music and dancing and eating and——"

"An' neckties to drink, Trot; don't forget the royal neckties," urged Cap'n Bill.

"We'll have all the fun there is going," continued the girl, "for we are to entertain the Army of the Pinkies."

"The Pinkies!" exclaimed the Captain of the Guards; "why, they're our enemies, your Short Highness."

"Not any more," replied Trot. "I'm Queen of the Pinkies, an' I'm also Queen of the Blues, so I won't have my people quarreling. Tell the Blue people we are to throw open the gates and welcome the Pinkies to the City, where everybody will join in a grand celebration. And jus' as soon as you've spread the news an' got the bands tuned up and the soldiers ready to march, you let us know and we'll head the procession."

"Your Microscopic Majesty shall be obeyed," said the Captain, and went away to carry out these commands.

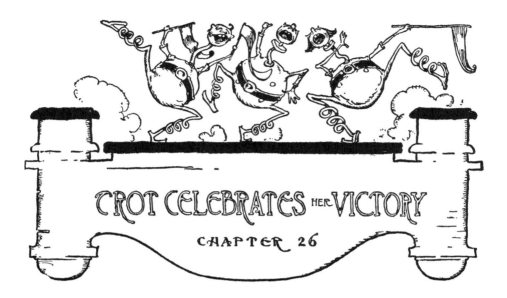

TROT CELEBRATES HER VICTORY

CHAPTER 26

THE Blue people were by this time dazed with wonder at all the events that had transpired that eventful day, but they still had wit enough to be glad the war was over; for in war some one is likely to get hurt and it is foolish to take such chances when one can remain quietly at home. The Blues did not especially admire the Pinkies, but it was easier to entertain them than to fight them, and, above all, the Blueskins were greatly rejoiced that their wicked Boolooroo had been conquered and could no longer abuse them. So they were quite willing to obey the orders of their girl Queen and in a short time the blasts of trumpets and roll of drums and clashing of cymbals told Trot and Cap'n Bill that the Blue Bands had assembled before the palace.

So they went down and found that a great crowd of people had gathered, and these cheered Trot with much enthusiasm

Chapter Twenty-Six

—which was very different from the scowls and surly looks with which they had formerly greeted their strange visitors from the Earth.

The soldiers wore their best blue uniforms and were formed before the palace in marching order, so Trot and Cap'n Bill headed the procession, and then came the soldiers —all keeping step—and then the bands, playing very loud noises on their instruments, and finally the crowd of Blue citizens waving flags and banners and shouting joyfully.

In this order they proceeded to the main gate, which Trot ordered the guards to throw wide open. Then they all marched out a little way into the fields and found that the Army of Pinkies had already formed and was advancing steadily toward them.

At the head of the Pinkies were Ghip-Ghisizzle and Button-Bright, who had the parrot on his shoulder, and they were supported by Captain Coralie and Captain Tintint and Rosalie the Witch. They had decided to capture the Blue City at all hazards, that they might rescue Trot and Cap'n Bill and conquer the Boolooroo, so when from a distance they saw the Blueskins march from the gate, with banners flying and bands playing, they supposed a most terrible fight was about to take place.

However, as the two forces came nearer together, Button-Bright spied Trot and Cap'n Bill standing before the enemy, and the sight astonished him considerably.

"Welcome, friends!" shouted Cap'n Bill in a loud voice; and "Welcome!" cried Trot; and "Welcome!" roared the Blue soldiers and the people of the Blue City.

"Hooray!" yelled the parrot,

"Welcome to our happy home
From which no longer will we roam!"

and then he flapped his wings and barked like a dog with pure delight, and added as fast as his bird's tongue could speak:

"One army's pink and one is blue,
But neither one is in a stew
Because the naughty Boolooroo
Is out of sight, so what we'll do
Is try to be a jolly crew
And dance and sing our too-ral-loo
And to our friends be ever true
And to our foes——"

"Stop it!" said Button-Bright; "I can't hear myself think."

The Pinkies were amazed at the strange reception of the Blues and hesitated to advance; but Trot now ran up in front of them and made a little speech.

Chapter Twenty-Six

"Pinkies," said she, "your Queen has conquered the Boolooroo and is now the Queen of the Blues. All of Sky Island, except the Fog Bank, is now my kingdom, so I welcome my faithful Pinkies to my Blue City, where you are to be royally entertained and have a good time. The war is over an' ever'body must be sociable an' happy or I'll know the reason why!"

Now, indeed, the Pinkies raised a great shout of joy and the Blues responded with another joyful shout, and Rosalie kissed the little girl and said she had performed wonders, and everybody shook hands with Cap'n Bill and congratulated him upon his escape, and the parrot flew to Trot's shoulder and screeched:

"The Pinkies are pink, the Blues are blue
But Trot's the Queen, so too-ral-loo!"

When the Blueskins saw Ghip-Ghisizzle they raised another great shout, for he was the favorite of the soldiers and very popular with all the people. But Ghip-Ghisizzle did not heed the shouting. He was looking downcast and sad, and it was easy to see he was disappointed because he had not conquered the Boolooroo himself. But the people called upon him for a speech, so he faced the Blueskins and said:

"I escaped from the City because the Boolooroo tried to patch me, as you all know, and the Six Snubnosed Princesses

255

tried to marry me, which would have been a far greater misfortune. But I have recovered the Book of Royal Records, which has long been hidden in the Treasure Chamber, and by reading it I find that the Boolooroo is not your lawful Boolooroo at all, having reigned more than his three hundred years. Since last Thursday, I, Ghip-Ghisizzle, have been the lawful Boolooroo of the Blue Country, but now that you are conquered by Queen Trot I suppose I am conquered, too, and you have no Boolooroo at all."

"Hooray!" cried the parrot;

"Here's a pretty howdy-do—
You haven't any Boolooroo!"

Trot had listened carefully to the Majordomo's speech. When he finished she said cheerfully:

"Don't worry, Sizzle dear; it'll all come right pretty soon. Now, then, let's enter the City an' enjoy the grand feast that's being cooked. I'm nearly starved, myself, for this conquerin' kingdoms is hard work."

So the Pinkies and the Blues marched side by side into the City and there was great rejoicing and music and dancing and feasting and games and merrymaking that lasted for three full days.

Trot carried Rosalie and Captain Coralie and Ghip-Ghisizzle to the palace, and of course Button-Bright and

Cap'n Bill were with her. They had the Royal Chef serve dinner at once and they ate it in great state, seated in the Royal Banquet Hall, where they were waited on by a hundred servants. The parrot perched upon the back of Queen Trot's chair and the girl fed it herself, being glad to have the jolly bird with her again.

After they had eaten all they could, and the servants had been sent away, Trot related her adventures, telling how, with the assistance of the billygoat, she had turned the tables on the wicked Boolooroo. Then she gave Rosalie back her magic ring, thanking the kind Witch for all she had done for them.

"And now," said she, "I want to say to Ghip-'Sizzle that jus' as soon as we can find Button-Bright's umbrel we're going to fly home again. I'll always be Queen of Sky Island, but the Pink and Blue Countries must each have a Ruler. I think I'll make 'Sizzle the Boolooroo of the Blues; but I want you to promise me, Ghip, that you'll destroy the Great Knife and its frame and clean up the room and turn it into a skating-rink an' never patch anyone as long as you rule the Blueskins."

Ghip-Ghisizzle was overjoyed at the prospect of being Boolooroo of the Blues, but he looked solemn at the promise Trot exacted.

"I'm not cruel," he said, "and I don't approve of patching in general, so I'll willingly destroy the Great Knife.

257

But before I do that I want the privilege of patching the Snubnosed Princesses to each other — mixing the six as much as possible — and then I want to patch the former Boolooroo to the billygoat, which is the same punishment he was going to inflict upon Cap'n Bill."

"No," said Trot, positively, "there's been enough patching in this country and I won't have any more of it. The old Boolooroo and the six stuck-up Princesses will be punished enough by being put out of the palace. The people don't like 'em a bit, so they'll be outcasts and wanderers and that will make 'em sorry they were so wicked an' cruel when they were powerful. Am I right, Cap'n Bill?"

"You are, mate," replied the sailor.

"Please, Queen Trot," begged Ghip-Ghisizzle, "let me patch just the Boolooroo. It will be such a satisfaction."

"I have said no, an' I mean it," answered the girl. "You let the poor old Boolooroo alone. There's nothing that hurts so much as a come-down in life, an' I 'spect the old rascal's goin' to be pretty miser'ble by'm'by."

"What does he say to his reverse of fortune?" asked Rosalie.

"Why, I don't b'lieve he knows about it," said Trot. "Guess I'd better send for him an' tell him what's happened."

So the Captain of the Guards was given the key and told to fetch the Boolooroo from the Room of the Great Knife. The guards had a terrible struggle with the goat, which was loose in the room and still wanted to fight, but finally they subdued the animal and then they took the Boolooroo out of the frame he was tied in and brought both him and the goat before Queen Trot, who awaited them in the throne room of the palace.

When the courtiers and the people assembled saw the goat they gave a great cheer, for the beast had helped to dethrone their wicked Ruler.

"What's goin' to happen to this tough ol' warrior, Trot?" asked Cap'n Bill. "It's my idee as he's braver than the whole Blue Army put together."

"You're right, Cap'n," she returned. "I'll have 'Sizzle make a fine yard for the goat, where he'll have plenty of blue grass to eat. An' I'll have a pretty fence put around it an' make all the people honor an' respec' him jus' as long as he lives."

"I'll gladly do that," promised the new Boolooroo; "and I'll feed the honorable goat all the shavings and leather and tin cans he can eat, besides the grass. He'll be the happiest goat in Sky Island, I assure you."

As they led the now famous animal from the room the Boolooroo shuddered and said:

"How dare you people give orders in my palace? I'm the Boolooroo!"

"'Scuse me," said Trot; "I neglected to tell you that you're not the Boolooroo any more. We've got the Royal

Record Book, an' it proves you've already ruled this country longer than you had any right to. 'Sides all that, I'm the Queen o' Sky Island—which means Queen o' the Pinkies an' Queen o' the Blues—both of 'em. So things are run as I say, an' I've made Ghip-Ghisizzle Boolooroo in your place. He'll look after this end of the Island hereafter, an' unless I'm much mistaken he'll do it a heap better than you did."

The former Boolooroo groaned.

"What's going to become of me, then?" he asked. "Am I to be patched, or what?"

"You won't be hurt," answered the girl, "but you'll have to find some other place to stay besides this palace, an' perhaps you'll enjoy workin' for a livin, by way of variety."

"Can't I take any of the treasure with me?" he pleaded.

"Not even a bird cage," said she. "Ever'thing in the palace now belongs to Ghip-Ghisizzle."

"Except the Six Snubnosed Princesses," exclaimed the new Boolooroo, earnestly. "Won't you please get rid of them, too, your Majesty? Can't they be discharged?"

"Of course," said Trot; "they must go with their dear father an' mother. Isn't there some house in the City they can all live in, Ghip?"

"Why, I own a little cabin at the end of the town," said Ghip-Ghisizzle, "and I'll let them use that, as I won't need it any longer. It isn't a very pretty cabin and the furniture is cheap and common, but I'm sure it is good enough for this wicked man and his family."

"I'll not be wicked any more," sighed the old Boolooroo; "I'll reform. It's always best to reform when it is no longer safe to remain wicked. As a private citizen I shall be a model of deportment, because it would be dangerous to be otherwise."

Trot now sent for the Princesses, who had been weeping and wailing and fighting among themselves ever since they learned that their father had been conquered. When first they entered the throne room they tried to be as haughty and scornful as ever, but the Blues who were assembled there all laughed at them and jeered them, for there was not a single person in all the Blue Country who loved the Princesses the least little bit.

Trot told the girls that they must go with their father to live in Ghip-Ghisizzle's little old cabin, and when they heard this dreadful decree the six snubnosed ones began to scream and have hysterics, and between them they managed to make so much noise that no one could hear anything else. So Ghip-Ghisizzle ordered the Captain to take a file of soldiers and escort the raving beauties to their new home.

This was done, the once royal family departing from the palace with shamed and downcast looks.

Then the Room of the Great Knife was cleared of its awful furniture. The frames were split into small pieces of bluewood, and the benches chopped into kindling, and the immense sharp knife broken into bits. All the rubbish was piled in the square before the palace and a bonfire made of it, while the Blue people clustered around and danced and sang with joy as the blue flames devoured the dreadful instrument that had once caused them so much unhappiness.

That evening Trot gave a grand ball in the palace, to which the most important of the Pinkies and the Blueskins were invited. The combined bands of both the countries played the music and a fine supper was served.

The Pinkies would not dance with the Blues, however, nor would the Blues dance with the Pinkies. The two nations were so different in all ways that they were unable to agree at all, and several times during the evening quarrels arose and there was fighting between them, which Trot promptly checked.

"I think it will be best for us to go back to our own country as soon as possible," suggested Rosalie the Witch; "for, if we stay here very long, the Blueskins may rise against us and cause the Pinkies much trouble."

"Jus' as soon as we find that umbrel," promised Trot, "we'll dive into the Fog Bank an' make tracks for the Land of Sunrise an' Sunset."

THE FATE OF THE MAGIC UMBRELLA
CHAPTER 27

NEXT morning the search for the Magic Umbrella began in earnest. With many to hunt for it and the liberty of the whole palace to aid them, every inch of the great building was carefully examined. But no trace of the umbrella could be found. Cap'n Bill and Button-Bright went down to the cabin of the former Boolooroo and tried to find out what he had done with the umbrella, but the old Boolooroo said:

"I had it brought from the Treasure Chamber and tried to make it work, but there was no magic about the thing. So I threw it away. I haven't any idea what became of it."

The six former Princesses were sitting upon a rude bench, looking quite bedraggled and untidy. Said Indigo:

"If you will make Ghip-Ghisizzle marry me, I'll find your old umbrella."

"Where is it?" asked Button-Bright, eagerly.

"Make Ghip-Ghisizzle marry me, and I'll tell you," repeated Indigo. "But I won't say another word about it until after I am married."

So they went back to the palace and proposed to the new Boolooroo to marry Indigo, so they could get their Magic Umbrella. But Ghip-Ghisizzle positively refused.

"I'd like to help you," said he, "but nothing will ever induce me to marry one of those snubnoses."

"They're very pretty — for Blueskins," said Trot.

"But when you marry a girl, you marry the inside as well as the outside," declared Ghip-Ghisizzle, "and inside these Princesses there are wicked hearts and evil thoughts. I'd rather be patched than marry the best of them."

"Which *is* the best?" asked Button-Bright.

"I don't know, I'm sure," was the reply. "Judging from their actions in the past, there is no best."

Rosalie the Witch now went to the cabin and put Indigo into a deep sleep, by means of a powerful charm. Then, while the Princess slept, the Witch made her tell all she knew, which wasn't a great deal, to be sure; but it was soon discovered that Indigo had been deceiving them and knew nothing at all about the umbrella. She had hoped to marry Ghip-Ghisizzle and become Queen, after which she could afford to laugh at their reproaches. So the Witch woke her up and went back to the palace to tell Trot of her failure.

The girl and Button-Bright and Cap'n Bill were all rather

discouraged by this time, for they had searched high and low and had not found a trace of the all-important umbrella. That night none of them slept much, for they all lay awake wondering how they could ever return to the Earth and to their homes.

In the morning of the third day after Trot's conquest of the Blues the little girl conceived another idea. She called all the servants of the palace to her and questioned them closely. But not one could remember having seen anything that looked like an umbrella.

"Are all the servants of the old Boolooroo here?" inquired Cap'n Bill, who was sorry to see Trot looking so sad and downcast.

"All but one," was the reply. "Tiggle used to be a servant, but he escaped and ran away."

"Oh, yes!" exclaimed Trot; "Tiggle is in hiding, somewhere. Perhaps he don't know there's been a revolution and a new Boolooroo rules the country. If he did, there's no need for him to hide any longer, for he is now in no danger."

She now dispatched messengers all through the City and the surrounding country, who cried aloud for Tiggle, saying that the new Boolooroo wanted him. Tiggle, hiding in the cellar of a deserted house in a back street, at last heard these cries and joyfully came forth to confront the messenger.

Having heard of the old Boolooroo's downfall and disgrace, the man consented to go to the palace again, and as soon as Trot saw him she asked about the umbrella.

Tiggle thought hard for a minute and then said he remembered sweeping the King's rooms and finding a queer thing—that might have been an umbrella—lying beneath

a cabinet. It had ropes and two wooden seats and a wicker basket all attached to the handle.

"That's it!" cried Button-Bright, excitedly; and "That's it!" "That's it!" cried both Trot and Cap'n Bill.

"But what did you do with it?" asked Ghip-Ghisizzle.

"I dragged it out and threw it on the rubbish heap, in an alley back of the palace," said Tiggle.

Chapter Twenty-Seven

At once they all rushed out to the alley and began digging in the rubbish heap. By and by Cap'n Bill uncovered the lunch basket, and pulling on this he soon drew up the two seats and, finally, the Magic Umbrella.

"Hurrah!" shouted Button-Bright, grabbing the umbrella and hugging it tight in his arms.

"Hooray!" shrieked the parrot;

"Cap'n Bill's a lucky fellah,
'Cause he found the old umbrella!"

Trot's face was wreathed in smiles.

"This is jus' the best luck that could have happened to us," she exclaimed, "'cause now we can go home whenever we please."

"Let's go now—this minute—before we lose the umbrella again," said Button-Bright.

But Trot shook her head.

"Not yet," she replied. "We've got to straighten out things in Sky Island, first of all. A Queen has some duties, you know, and as long as I'm Queen here I've got to live up to the part."

"What has to be did, mate?" inquired Cap'n Bill.

"Well, we've fixed the Blue Country pretty well, by makin' 'Sizzle the Boolooroo of it; but the Pinkies mus' be looked after, too, 'cause they've stood by us an' helped us to win. We must take 'em home again, safe an' sound, and get a new Queen to rule over'em. When that's done we can go home any time we want to."

"Quite right, Trot," said the sailor, approvingly. "When do we march?"

"Right away," she replied. "I've had enough of the Blue Country. Haven't you?"

"We have, mate."

"We've had plenty of it," observed Button-Bright.

"And the Pinkies are anxious to get home," added Rosalie, who was present.

So Cap'n Bill unhooked the seats from the handle of the umbrella and wound the ropes around the two boards and made a package of them, which he carried under his arm. Trot took the empty lunch-basket and Button-Bright held fast to the precious umbrella. Then they returned to the palace to bid good-bye to Ghip-Ghisizzle and the Blues.

The new Boolooroo seemed rather sorry to lose his friends, but the people were secretly glad to get rid of the strangers, especially of the Pinkies. They maintained a sullen silence while Coralie and Captain Tintint formed their ranks in marching order, and they did not even cheer when Trot said to them in a final speech:

"I'm the Queen of Sky Island, you know, and the new Boolooroo has got to carry out my orders and treat you all nicely while I'm away. I don't know when I'll come back, but you'd better watch out an' not make any trouble, or I'll find a way to make you sorry for it. So now, good-bye!"

"And good riddance!" screamed the Six Snubnosed Girls who had once been Princesses, and who were now in the crowd that watched the departure.

But Trot paid no attention to them. She made a signal to the Pinkie Band, which struck up a fine Pink March, and then the Army stepped out with the left foot first, and away went the conquerers down the streets of the Blue City, out of the blue-barred gateway and across the country toward the Fog Bank.

THE ELEPHANT'S HEAD COMES TO LIFE

CHAPTER 28

WHEN they reached the edge of the Fog Bank the Pinkies all halted to put on their raincoats and Button-Bright put up his umbrella and held it over himself and Trot. Then, when everybody was ready, they entered the Fog and Rosalie the Witch made a signal to call the Frog King and his subjects to aid them, as they had done before.

Pretty soon the great frogs appeared, a long line of them facing Trot and her Pink Army and sitting upon their haunches close together.

"Turn around, so we can get upon your backs," said Rosalie.

"Not yet," answered the Frog King, in a gruff, deep voice. "You must first take that insulting umbrella out of my dominions."

Chapter Twenty-Eight

"Why, what is there about my umbrella that seems insulting?" asked Button-Bright, in surprise.

"It is an insinuation that you don't like our glorious climate, and object to our delightful fog, and are trying to ward off its soulful, clinging kisses," replied the Frog King, in an agitated voice. "There has never been an umbrella in my kingdom before, and I'll not allow one in it now. Take it away at once!"

"But we can't," explained Trot. "We've got to take the umbrella with us to the Pink Country. We'll put it down, if you like, an' cross the bank in this drizzle — which may be clingin' an' soulful, but is too wet to be comfort'ble. But the umbrella's got to go with us."

"It can't go another inch," cried the obstinate frog, with an angry croak, "nor shall any of your people advance another step while that insulting umbrella is with you."

Trot turned to Rosalie.

"What shall we do?" she asked.

"I really do not know," replied the Witch, greatly perplexed.

"Can't you *make* the frogs let us through?" inquired the boy.

"No; I have no power over the frogs," Rosalie answered. "They carried us before as a favor, but if the king now insists that we cannot pass with the umbrella we must go back to the Blue Country or leave your umbrella behind us."

"We won't do that!" said Button-Bright, indignantly. "Can't we fight the frogs?"

"Fight!" cried Trot; "why, see how big they are. They could eat up our whole army, if they wanted to."

But just then, while they stood dismayed at this unfortunate position, a queer thing happened. The umbrella in

Button-Bright's hand began to tremble and shake. He looked down at the handle and saw that the red eyes of the carved elephant's head were rolling fiercely and sending out red sparks of anger in all directions. The trunk swayed from side to side and the entire head began to swell and grow larger.

Chapter Twenty-Eight

In his fright the boy sprang backward a step and dropped the umbrella to the ground, and as he did so it took the form of a complete elephant, growing rapidly to a monstrous size. Then, flapping its ears and wagging its tail—which was merely the covered frame of the umbrella—the huge elephant lifted its trunk and charged the line of astonished frogs.

In a twinkling the frogs all turned and made the longest leaps their powerful legs enabled them to. The King jumped first of all and in a panic of fear the others followed his example. They were out of sight in an instant, and then the elephant turned its head and looked at Button-Bright and at once trotted into the depths of the fog.

"He wants us to follow," said the boy, gasping in amazement at this wonderful transformation. So immediately they began marching through the fog behind the elephant, and as the great beast advanced the frogs scrambled out of his way and hid themselves in the moist banks until he had passed them by.

Cap'n Bill had to mind his wooden leg carefully and the old sailor was so excited that he mumbled queer sentences about "Araby Ann Knights," and "ding-donged magic" and the "fool foolishness of fussin' with witches an' sich," until Trot wondered whether her old friend had gone crazy or was only badly scared.

It was a long journey, and all the Pinkies were dripping

water from their raincoats, and their little fat legs were tired and aching, when the pink glow showing through the fog at last announced the fact that they were nearing the Pink Country.

At the very edge of the Fog Bank the elephant halted, winked at Button-Bright, lowered its head and began to shrink in size and dwindle away. By the time the boy came up to it, closely followed by Trot and Cap'n Bill, the thing was only the well-known Magic Umbrella, with the carved elephant's head for a handle, and it lay motionless upon the ground. Button-Bright cautiously picked it up and as he examined it he thought the tiny red eyes still twinkled a little, as if with triumph and pride.

Trot drew a long breath.

"That was *some* magic, I guess!" she exclaimed. "Don't you think so, Rosalie?"

"It was the most wonderful thing I ever saw," admitted the Witch. "The fairies who control Button-Bright's umbrella must be very powerful, indeed!"

274

CROT REGULATES THE PINKIES

CHAPTER 29.

THE Pinkies were rejoiced to find themselves again in their beloved land of sunrises and sunsets. They sang and shouted with glee and the Band uncovered its pink instruments and played the National Pink Anthem, while the parrot flew from Trot's shoulder to Cap'n Bill's shoulder and back again, screaming ecstatically:

"Hooray! we're through the wetful fogs
  Where the elephant scared the fretful frogs!"

There was a magnificent sunset in the sky just then and it cheered the Pinkies and gave them renewed strength. Away they hastened across the pink fields to the Pink City, where all the Pink people who had been left behind ran out to welcome them home again.

275

Trot and Button-Bright, with Cap'n Bill and Rosalie the Witch, went to the humble palace, where they had a simple supper of coarse food and slept upon hard beds. In the houses of the City, however, there was much feasting and merry-making, and it seemed to Trot that the laws of the country which forbade the Queen from enjoying all the good things the people did were decidedly wrong and needed changing.

The next morning Rosalie said to the little girl:

"Will you make Tourmaline the Queen again, when you go away?"

"I'll send for her and see about it," replied Trot.

But when Tourmaline arrived at the palace, dressed all in lovely fluffy robes and with a dainty pink plume in her pink hair, she begged most earnestly not to be made the Queen again.

"I'm having a good time, just now, after years of worry and uncomfortable living in this uncomfortable old hut of a palace," said the poor girl, "so it would be cruel for you to make me the servant of the people again and condemn me to want and misery."

"That seems reason'ble," replied Trot, thoughtfully.

"Rosalie's skin is just as light a pink as my own," continued Tourmaline. "Why don't you make her the Queen?"

"I hadn't thought of that," said Trot. Then she turned to Rosalie and asked: "How would you like to rule the Pinkies?"

Chapter Twenty-Nine

"I wouldn't like it," replied the Witch, with a smile. "The Queen is the poorest and most miserable creature in all the kingdom and I'm sure I don't deserve such a fate. I've always tried to be a good witch and to do my duty."

Trot thought this over quite seriously for a time. Then one of her quaint ideas came to her—so quaint that it was entirely sensible.

"I'm the Queen of the Pinkies just now, am I not?" she asked.

"Of course," answered Rosalie; "none can dispute that."

"Then I've the right to make new laws, haven't I?"

"I believe so."

"In that case," said the girl, "I'm goin' to make a law that the Queen shall have the same food an' the same dresses an' the same good times that her people have; and she shall live in a house jus' as good as the houses of any of her people, an' have as much money to spend as anybody. But no more. The Queen can have her share of ever'thing, 'cordin' to the new law, but if she tries to get more than her share I'll have the law say she shall be taken to the edge an' pushed off. What do you think of *that* law, Rosalie?"

"It's a good law, and a just one," replied the Witch approvingly.

So Trot sent for the Royal Scribbler, who was a very fat Pinky with large pink eyes and curly pink hair, and had him carefully write the new law in the Great Book of Laws. The

Royal Scribbler wrote it very nicely in pink ink, with a big capital letter at the beginning and a fine flourish at the end. After Trot had signed her name to it as Queen she called all of the important people of the land to assemble in the Court of the Statues and ordered the Royal Declaimer to read to them the new law. The Pinkies seemed to think it was a just law and much better than the old one, and Rosalie said:

"Now no one can object to becoming the Queen, since the Ruler of the Pinkies will no longer be obliged to endure suffering and hardships."

"All right," said Trot. "In that case I'll make you the Queen, Rosalie, for you've got more sense than Tourmaline has and your powers as a witch will help you to protect the people."

At once she made the announcement, telling the assembled Pinkies that by virtue of her high office as Queen of Sky Island she would leave Rosalie the Witch to rule over the Pink Country while she returned to the Earth with her friends. As Rosalie was greatly loved and respected, the people joyfully accepted her as their Queen, and Trot ordered them to tear down the old hut and build a new palace for Rosalie—one which would be just as good as any other house in the City, but no better. She further ordered a pink statue of Tourmaline to be set up in the Court, and also a pink statue of herself, so that the record of all the rulers of the Pinkies should be complete.

Chapter Twenty-Nine

The people agreed to do all this as soon as possible, and some of the leaders whispered together and then asked Coralie to be their spokeman in replying to Queen Trot's speech.

Coralie stood on a chair and made a bow, after which she thanked Trot in the name of the Pinkies for leading them safely into the Blue Country and out again, and for giving them so good a Queen as Rosalie. The Pinkies would be sorry to have their new friends, the Earth people, leave them, but asked the Queen of Sky Island to carry with her the royal band of pink gold which she now wore upon her brow, together with the glistening pink jewel set in its center. It would remind her, Coralie declared, of the Beautiful Land of Sunset and Sunrise and of the fact that the Pinkies would always be glad to welcome her back.

Trot knew she would never return to Sky Island, but she did not tell them that. She merely thanked Coralie and the Pinkies and said they might all come to the Court after dinner and see her and her comrades fly away through the sky.

THE JOURNEY HOME.

CHAPTER 30.

AFTER the Pinkies had been dismissed, their new Queen Rosalie, by means of a clever charm, conjured up a dinner table set with very nice things to eat. They all enjoyed a hearty meal and afterward sat and talked over their adventures.

"Will you take the parrot home with you, Trot?" asked Cap'n Bill.

"Guess not, Cap'n," she answered. "Mother wouldn't like to have him hangin' 'round an' screechin' bad po'try ev'ry minute. I'll give him to Rosalie, for I'm sure she'll take good care of him."

Rosalie accepted the gift with pleasure, but the parrot looked sober awhile and then said:

Chapter Thirty

"This looks to me like a give-away;
But here I am, and here I'll stay.
The country's pink, but we'll all be blue
When Trot goes home, as she says she'll do."

They now packed the lunch-basket with the remains of the feast, for they knew a long journey was before them and feared they might be hungry before they landed again. Cap'n Bill straightened out the ropes and adjusted the seats, while Button-Bright examined the umbrella to see if it had been injured in any way when the elephant tramped through the Fog Bank.

The boy looked into the small red eyes of the carved elephant's-head handle with some misgivings, but as seen in the strong sunshine the eyes were merely red stones, while the handle plainly showed the marks of the tool that had carved it.

When all was ready they went into the Court of the Statues, where all the Pinkies were assembled—together with their Pink Band—and Cap'n Bill hooked the swinging seats onto the handle of the Magic Umbrella.

Trot kissed Rosalie and Coralie and Tourmaline goodbye and said to them:

"If you ever happen to come to Earth you must be sure to visit me and I'll try to give you a good time. But p'raps you'll stay here all your lives."

"I think we shall," replied Rosalie, laughing, "for in all Sky Island there will be no Magic Umbrella for us to fly with."

"And when you see Polychrome," added Trot, "jus' give her my love."

Then she and Button-Bright seated themselves in the double seat, which was flat upon the pink ground, and Cap'n Bill sat before them on his own seat, to which the lunch basket had been fastened by means of a stout cord.

"Hold fast!" said the sailorman, and they all held fast to the ropes while the boy, glancing up toward the open umbrella he held, said solemnly and distinctly:

"Take us to Trot's house on the Earth."

The umbrella obeyed, at once mounting into the air. It moved slowly at first but gradually increased its speed. First it lifted the seat of the boy and girl, then Cap'n Bill's seat and finally the lunch-basket.

"Fly high!—mind your eye!
Don't cry!—bye-bye!"

shouted the parrot from the Pink Witch's shoulder.

Trot leaned over and waved her hand. The Pink Band played as loud as it could—in order that the travelers might hear it as long as possible—and Rosalie and Coralie and Tourmaline threw kisses to their vanishing friends as long as they remained in sight.

* * * * * * * * *

Chapter Thirty

"Seems good to be on the way home again," remarked Trot, as the umbrella bumped into a big black cloud.

"It reely does, mate," answered the sailorman, joyously.

Fast through the cloud the umbrella swept and then suddenly it sailed into a clear blue sky, across which a great and gorgeous Rainbow spread its radiant arch. Upon the bow danced the dainty Daughters of the Rainbow, and the umbrella passed near enough to it for the passengers to observe Polychrome merrily leading her sisters, her fleecy robes waving prettily in the gentle breeze.

"Good-bye, Polly!" cried Button-Bright, and Trot and Cap'n Bill both called out: "Good-bye!"

Polychrome heard and nodded to them smilingly, never halting in her graceful dance. Then the umbrella dropped far below the arch, which presently faded from view.

It was an exciting ride. Scenes presented themselves entirely different from those they had seen on their former voyage, for the sky changes continually and the clouds of the moment are not the clouds of an hour ago. Once they passed between two small stars as brilliant as diamonds, and once an enormous bird, whose wings spread so wide that they shadowed the sun, soared directly over them and lost itself in the vague distance of the limitless sky.

They rode quite comfortably, however, and were full of eager interest in what they saw. The rush of air past them made them hungry, so Cap'n Bill drew up the lunch-basket

283

and held it so that Button-Bright and Trot could help themselves to the pink food, which tasted very good. And, finally, a dark rim appeared below them, which the sailor declared must be the Earth. He proved to be correct and when they came nearer they found themselves flying over the waves of the ocean. Pretty soon a small island appeared, and Trot exclaimed:

"That's the Sky Island we thought we were goin' to— only we didn't."

"Yes; an' there's the mainland, mate!" cried Cap'n Bill excitedly, pointing toward a distant coast.

On swept the Magic Umbrella. Then its speed gradually slackened; the houses and trees on the coast could be seen, and presently—almost before they realized it—they were set down gently upon the high bluff near the giant acacia. A little way off stood the white cottage where Trot lived.

It was growing dusk as Cap'n Bill unhooked the seats and Button-Bright folded up the umbrella and tucked it under his arm. Trot seized the lunch-basket and ran to the house, where she found her mother busy in the kitchen.

"Well, I'm back again," said the little girl. "Is supper ready, mama?"

Button-Bright stayed all night with them, but next morning, bright and early, he hooked one of the seats to his Magic Umbrella, said good-bye to Trot and Cap'n Bill and flew into the air to begin his journey to Philadelphia. Just before he started Trot said:

"Let me know if you get home safe, Button-Bright; an' come an' see me again as quick as you can."

"I'll try to come again," said the boy. "We've had a good time; haven't we, Trot?"

"The bes' time I *ever* had!" she replied, enthusiastically. Then she asked: "Didn't you like it, too, Cap'n Bill?"

"Parts o' it, mate," the sailor answered, as he thoughtfully made marks in the sand with the end of his wooden leg; "but seems to me the bes' part of all was gett'n' home again."

Sky Island

After several days Trot received a postal-card from But-ton-Bright. It was awkwardly scrawled, for the boy was not much of a writer, but Trot managed to make out the words. It read as follows:

"Got home safe, Trot, and the folks were so worried they forgot to scold me. Father has taken the Magic Umbrella and locked it up in a big strong chest in the attic. He put the key in his own pocket, so I don't know as I'll ever be able to see you again. But I'll never forget the Queen of Sky Island, and I send my love to you and Cap'n Bill.

Your friend,

BUTTON-BRIGHT."

THE END.